D0345210

MARGARET
AND THE
MOTH TREE

MARGARET
AND THE
MOTH TREE

BY **BRIT TROGEN** AND **KARI TROGEN**

KIDS CAN PRESS

Kids Can Press acknowledges the financial support of the Government of Ontario,
through the Ontario Media Development Corporation's Ontario Book Initiative;
the Ontario Arts Council; the Canada Council for the Arts; and the Government
of Canada, through the BPIDP, for our publishing activity.

Published in Canada by
Kids Can Press Ltd.
25 Dockside Drive
Toronto, ON M5A 0B5

Published in the U.S. by
Kids Can Press Ltd.
2250 Military Road
Tonawanda, NY 14150

www.kidscanpress.com

Edited by Sheila Barry
Designed by Marie Bartholomew
Cover illustration by Elly MacKay

This book is smyth sewn casebound.
Manufactured in Altona, Manitoba,
Canada, in 12/2011 by Friesens Corporation

FSC
www.fsc.org

MIX
Paper from
responsible sources
FSC® C016245

CM 12 0 9 8 7 6 5 4 3 2 1

Library and Archives Canada Cataloguing in Publication

Trogen, Brit
   Margaret and the moth tree / written by Brit Trogen and
Kari Trogen.

ISBN 978-1-55453-823-2

   I. Trogen, Kari II. Title.

PS8639.R64M37 2012   jC813'.6   C2011-905933-9

Kids Can Press is a **l☺n∪s**™ Entertainment company

CONTENTS

For Janet, who raised us on books,
and our grandma, Vera, who loved to write
— B.T. and K.T.

PART ONE

THE FOUNDLING

CHAPTER 1

THE SAD HOUSE

If this were a proper world, beautiful faces would belong to beautiful people.

Good people with kind hearts and clever minds would always have bright eyes and dazzling smiles, and bad people would have scraggly hair and warty noses. That way if you saw one of *them* coming, you could cross to the other side of the street and avoid them altogether.

But this is not a proper world. In our world, many bad people look quite nice, and many good people are not beautiful at all. Many good people aren't pretty or cute or even interesting-looking.

A very small girl named Margaret Grey was one of these.

"I don't want her," said a woman with thick spectacles and white hair pinned up in a bun.

"I don't want her either," said a man with dirty fingernails.

The reason Margaret was so small was that she was

a toddler, though as toddlers go, she was not a very adorable one. She had plain brown hair and plain brown eyes and a plain little face that gave no hint that, even at one-and-a-half, she was both kindhearted and clever. She was the type of child most people would call *unremarkable*.

She was sitting on the floor of a very sad house. The man and the woman were staring down at her, and Margaret, who was holding a rattle, was staring back.

The house was called Grey Cottage and it had a large sign on its front door that said: FORECLOSED BY THE BANK. It was really quite a nice house, aside from the sign, and it hadn't always been a sad place. Until recently it had belonged to a couple called Anthony and Lillian Grey, and until recently this couple had been Margaret's parents.

Anthony and Lillian Grey were the type of parents you might wish for when your own are acting un-reasonable. They took Margaret to the petting zoo and put on shadow puppet shows and made up stories with funny voices.

But here is where the sadness comes in. Anthony and Lillian Grey had recently perished in a freak car accident.

Grey Cottage no longer belonged to anyone. Two burly men were carrying bookcases and potted plants out its front door. And young Margaret was looking from one strange grown-up to the other, wondering which of them was going to take care of her.

"You'll have to take her," said the woman, who was called Great-aunt Linda.

"I'm unfamiliar with toddlers," said the man, who was called Cousin Amos.

"Don't talk back to me. I'm old, and old people must be humored," said the woman, meaning that sometimes you have to do what old people tell you to keep them from getting snippy.

It is true that old people must be humored, just as it is true that small toddlers must be housed somewhere. So the grumbling man called Amos took Margaret by the hand, and that was that.

CHAPTER 2

A LACK OF GREYS

If you are very lucky and have had a more-or-less enjoyable life, you may not know much about lack.

Lack is a way of saying that you're missing something important. Margaret, for example, lacked parents, which meant she had to live with Cousin Amos. And Cousin Amos lacked a great many things.

He lived in a creaky old house covered in peeling paint, with a garden full of prickly weeds. His house lacked many of the things that toddlers need, like cuddly teddy bears and childproof corners and personal hygiene.

Amos was a lifelong bachelor, which meant he never cooked or cleaned at all if he could avoid it. His kitchen was foul, his bathroom was even worse, and he hadn't washed his socks in three years.

But the thing that was most lacking in Cousin Amos's house was conversation. Amos dreaded talking, and he never spoke to anyone unless he absolutely had to. Even then, he would limit himself to talking about vegetables or economics, because years of experience had taught him that these topics were guaranteed to put a stop to any conversation and allow him to return to his favorite habit of not talking.

So when Amos became Margaret's guardian, her small vocabulary of the words "dada," "moose" and "eggplant" became completely unnecessary.

Instead of saying, "Please pass the brussels sprouts" at meal times, Amos would point and grunt.

Instead of saying, "Good night, Margaret. Don't let the bedbugs bite" at bedtime, Amos would pat her twice on the head and turn off the lights.

And instead of saying, "I'm so sorry about your parents. Is there anything I can do to make you feel better?" Amos didn't think to say anything at all.

When you spend a lot of time in a perfectly quiet house surrounded by perfectly quiet people, you have little choice but to be very quiet yourself. This is just what happened to Margaret Grey.

Without any brothers or sisters or playmates to shout and scream and holler with, Margaret didn't do the shouting and screaming and hollering that most children do. When she talked with the milkman on the step each morning, he could never stay long before continuing on his way. When she whispered to the German nanny over breakfast, the most she ever got in return was a nod or a close-lipped smile. And as soon as Margaret seemed old enough to look after herself, Amos got rid of the nanny altogether, and Margaret's world grew quieter still.

The life of a quiet girl in a quiet house may not seem a very remarkable thing. But Margaret learned something in Amos's house that very few people know how to do: Margaret learned how to listen.

You probably think that you know how to listen and, in a way, you are right. You know how to listen to the radio, or to someone singing in the shower. But Margaret's kind of listening was not the usual kind. Margaret learned how to *really truly* listen, which is something that very few people ever come to do.

By the time she was four years old, Margaret could hear things that even excellent listeners have trouble detecting, like a barn owl swooping through the air and the sound of the neighbor's cat yawning.

At four and a half, she could hear leaves falling in the yard and a mouse behind the wall chewing a bit of cheese.

And by the age of five, she could hear things that only a few people in the world have ever heard, like a shadow creeping across the floorboards, and the first rays of sunlight as they passed through the window.

It is entirely possible that with a few more years of practice, Margaret could even have learned to listen to the very deepest and most secret thoughts that dance through people's minds.

But this is not what happened. Because shortly after Margaret's fifth birthday, when Cousin Amos died suddenly of antisanitosis, Margaret went to live with Great-aunt Linda. And from that point on, her life became very different.

"I never thought I'd have to spend my golden years looking after a child," Great-aunt Linda said the first time she shooed Margaret through her door. "Life is full of surprises."

"I'm sorry, Auntie," said Margaret.

Great-aunt Linda was an old maid, which is exactly the opposite of a lifelong bachelor. Her house was spick and span, with fancy pillows on every chair and lacy tablecloths on every table and half a dozen hypoallergenic cats. And unlike Cousin Amos, who said hardly anything at all, Great-aunt Linda liked the sound of her own voice. She was especially fond of neat little phrases that don't really mean anything, like "life is full of surprises."

"Idle hands are the devil's playthings," she said on the morning of Margaret's arrival, handing her a piece of embroidery.

"Too many cooks spoil the broth," she said on her way to play backgammon, shooing Margaret into the kitchen to make soup.

"Children should be seen and not heard," she said when Margaret opened her mouth to say that she'd never made soup.

And so it was that instead of a house filled with quiet, Margaret found herself in a house filled with the mews of six hairless cats and the endless chattering of her great-aunt.

Great aunt Linda taught Margaret to read using passages from her favorite etiquette books, and gave her weekly quizzes on topics like "The Art of Polite Conversation" and "Forks and Their Uses." As a reward for perfect marks, Margaret was taken to backgammon night, where other old ladies gave her butter tarts in the corner of a stuffy room.

As time went by, Margaret grew into a very polite little girl, but the marvelous listening skills that she'd had in Amos's house became rusty.

When she tried to listen for the first rays of sunlight, all she could hear was the mewing of cats.

When she tried to listen to the falling autumn leaves, they were drowned out by Great-aunt Linda's favorite radio drama.

And she soon stopped listening altogether.

You see, any talent that isn't used will eventually be lost. By the time Margaret reached her sixth birthday, she could no longer hear any of the quiet sounds that had once filled her small world. And by the time Great-aunt Linda died of old age four years later, Margaret had forgotten that she'd ever heard them at all.

CHAPTER 3

THE C.L.C.

After Great-aunt Linda's funeral, the backgammon ladies herded Margaret out the church door, told her to mind her manners and shooed her onto a crowded bus.

"Going to Hopeton, eh?" asked her seatmate, a wrinkled old man who smelled faintly of cough drops. "To that charity—what's it called? The Worried Women's Group, or something?"

Margaret nodded, grabbing hold of the seat in front of her as the bus lurched forward. As she settled into her seat and the man settled into a coughing fit, she had the chance, for the first time in many days, to think about her situation.

Margaret now lacked a great many things a young girl should have. She had no home, no family, and no possessions save for a ratty tweed bag that had once belonged to Cousin Amos. Her hair was a mess of knots, as no one had thought to comb it in three days, and the tight black dress she had worn to the funeral pinched painfully under the arms.

Some people in Margaret's place might sit around feeling sorry for themselves, but if she had learned anything from Great-aunt Linda it was that well-brought-up people should always "keep a stiff upper lip." This was Linda's way of saying that you should just get on with things instead of moping. So as Margaret was jerked and jostled and coughed on during that long and uncomfortable ride, she tried her best to feel hopeful about what lay ahead.

After several cramped and bumpy hours, the bus came to a stop.

"C.L.C.," said the driver. "That's you," he added, bobbing his head at Margaret, who made her way to the front of the bus.

Stepping out onto the sidewalk, she looked around. She was standing on a quiet street of narrow buildings, trimly painted in pastel yellows, peaches and blues. There was no one in sight, but the building directly in front of her stood out from the rest.

It was smart red brick, and hanging over its door was a sign. On the sign there were large curlicue letters that read: THE CONCERNED LADIES' CLUB. And below them, in smaller letters: *Finding a Home for the Pitiful Foundling, for over Thirty-Seven Years.* As Margaret stared up at the sign, her eyes fixed themselves on four letters: H-O-M-E.

Taking a deep breath, she walked up the steps,

stretched onto the tips of her toes and knocked on the door with a large bronze door knocker that was carved in the shape of a hand.

"Yes?" said a voice, though there didn't seem to be anybody there.

"Hello?" said Margaret.

"Who's there?" said the voice, and Margaret realized it was coming from a mail slot set into the door. She stretched up to look through the slot and saw a pair of large bulgy eyes peering back at her.

"I'm Margaret Grey," she told the eyes. "I'd like a home, please."

The eyes narrowed. "Are you a foundling?" asked the voice.

"I think so," Margaret said.

"Are you pitiful?" The eyes bulged even more as they stared down at her knotted hair and ratty tweed bag.

"I suppose," Margaret said.

The eyes disappeared, and the mail slot snapped shut. A moment later Margaret heard the scraping of locks being turned, and the door swung open to reveal a short, dumpy old lady wearing a lacy pink dress. In addition to bulgy eyes, she had bluish-gray hair that was pinned up in tight curls all over her head. She smiled a toothy smile.

"Welcome," she said, "to the Concerned Ladies' Club!"

Margaret smiled back.

"Follow me," the lady said.

Margaret followed her down a narrow hallway. They

came to a room with a desk, and sitting behind the desk was another elderly lady, this one wearing a purple pantsuit.

"I found one!" said the dumpy lady.

The lady behind the desk looked up. She was thin and birdlike, with large glasses and a long pointy nose.

"*Procedure*, Prudence," she said, looking concerned.

"Oops!" said the dumpy lady, who was called Prudence. "I almost forgot." Taking hold of Margaret's sleeve, she cleared her throat noisily. "Admission request for one Pitiful Foundling to the care of the C.L.C."

"Granted," said the birdlike lady. She stared at Margaret over the tops of her glasses. "Hmph," she said. "I suppose she'll do. Leave us, Prudie."

Prudie bobbed her head and set off back down the hall.

The birdish lady pointed at one of the chairs. "Sit," she said.

Margaret sat.

The lady took a sheet of paper from one of the desk drawers. "Name?" she asked, without looking up.

"Margaret Grey," Margaret said.

The lady peered up over the tops of her glasses. "With whom were you staying before now?"

"My Great-aunt Linda."

"Hmph," said the lady, scribbling on the paper. "And where is your Great-aunt Linda now? Tired of taking care of you, I suppose. Probably gone on vacation to the Netherlands."

"No," Margaret said. "She died."

"Hmph," the lady said again, as if that was a very inconsiderate thing for a person to do. "What are your ambitions in the world?"

"I beg your pardon?" said Margaret.

"Your *ambitions*, girl," said the lady. "Surely you don't intend to be a silly little child for the rest of your life. I, for example, started my career in knitting then moved into philanthropy. What do you intend to do?"

"I don't know," said Margaret.

"Tsk," said the lady, shaking her head. She jotted something down on the paper. "Well, you ought to be very grateful. We've got a place for you at the Hopeton Orphanage."

"Oh," said Margaret, who didn't feel especially grateful but tried her best to look it. "Thank you."

But the birdlike lady wasn't listening. "Han-nah!" she shouted suddenly, peering out the office door. "Han-nah!"

After a moment another woman appeared in the room. She wasn't dumpy like the woman who'd answered the door, or birdish like the woman at the desk. She wasn't very old or very young. In fact, if you were seeing her for the first time you wouldn't think there was anything really remarkable about her at all, unless you looked into her hazel eyes and saw the depth of kindness there.

"Hannah," said the birdlike lady. "Prepare the car. We are taking Marjorie to her new home."

"Margaret," corrected Margaret.

"Hmph," said the birdlike lady.

The unremarkable face of the lady named Hannah blossomed into a warm smile. "How wonderful!" she said, her voice as soft as feathers. "It's a pleasure to meet you, Margaret. I'm Hannah Tender."

Hannah's hazel eyes met Margaret's brown ones. And though Margaret still knew she was alone in the world, she felt somehow a little safer.

"Yes, yes," said the birdlike lady. "Follow *procedure*, please, Hannah. The car."

"Right away, Gertrude." Hannah gave Margaret another warm smile, then hurried from the room.

"Very well, child," continued the birdlike lady, whose name, it appeared, was Gertrude. "I assume you don't need anything else."

Margaret was tired, hungry and rather in need of a good scrubbing, but not wanting to be a bother, she shook her head politely.

"Good," said Gertrude. "I'll telephone Miss Switch, then, and we'll be off."

And before Margaret could ask who Miss Switch might be, Gertrude had shooed her out into the hallway and shut the door.

CHAPTER 4

THE ORPHANAGE

If there has ever been a time in your life when you have wanted something to come right away, like Christmas morning, or your birthday, or the day you will no longer be alone in the world, then you know that the more you want something to hurry up and arrive, the longer it is likely to take.

And so, as Margaret gazed out the window of a shining pink car, watching the streets of the town give way to trees and rolling hills, the drive to the Hopeton Orphanage seemed to last forever.

"Don't daydream, child," said Gertrude, who was driving the car. "It causes warts."

"That it does," agreed Prudie, who was in the front seat.

"You must be nervous," whispered Hannah, who was sitting next to Margaret in the back of the car.

"Keep your head squarely on your shoulders," Gertrude continued.

"There's nothing like lemon juice to get rid of warts," said Prudie.

"Yes," Margaret whispered back, staring up at Hannah. "I just hope they like me."

Hannah smiled. "They'll love you," she whispered. And then, as if she were reading Margaret's mind, "Don't worry, we're almost there."

Sure enough, only a few minutes later, the dirt road carried them over the top of a hill. "There!" breathed Hannah, pointing off in the distance.

Margaret caught her breath. At the end of the road was an enormous white gabled house. Wide windows shone across the front of the building in the light of the sun, and a gleaming porch circled around it.

As they came nearer, Margaret saw that children wearing lovely red and blue coveralls were playing on the porch steps, which had bushes of budding roses on the lawn at either side. The children were smiling, and they waved happily at the car as it approached.

"Here we are," said Gertrude. "The Hopeton Orphanage."

Margaret's Great-aunt Linda had often said, "You should never judge a book by its cover." This is very difficult advice to follow, as the cover of a book can often tell you a great deal about whether or not it is something you might want to read.

If you saw a book with a plain white cover that was called *An Introduction to Economics*, you would likely put it down and walk away. But if the book had a colorful picture on the front and was called something delightful like *The Mystery of the Dragon's Egg* or *Adventures on Jungle Rock Island*, you would probably snatch it off the shelf in an instant.

So you can hardly blame Margaret, when she saw the enormous house that was to be her home and the happy children who were to be her friends, for judging that the Hopeton Orphanage was going to be a wonderful place to live.

Gertrude pulled the car around in a wide circle and came to a stop. Just then, the front door of the house swung open and a woman stepped out.

If Margaret had been excited before, she now felt close to bursting. Because her first impression of this woman was that she was the most beautiful person Margaret had ever seen.

The woman was tall, with silky golden hair and creamy skin. She was wearing a plain gray dress with a tattered flower-print apron tied around her waist, and a dusting of flour was brushed lightly across her hands and one cheek.

When she looked up and saw the car, her face broke into a dazzling smile.

The children parted before her as she descended the steps, and Gertrude, Prudie and Hannah climbed out of the car.

"Gertrude, Prudence!" said the woman, wiping her hands on her apron and waving at them.

"Miss Switch!" said Gertrude. "How nice to see you again."

"Hello, Hannah," said Miss Switch, with a small nod. "And this must be our new arrival."

She opened Margaret's door and leaned down so that they were eye to eye.

"Hello, darling!"

"Hello," said Margaret, feeling dizzy. The beautiful woman smelled like fresh baked bread, and she was looking into Margaret's eyes exactly as Margaret had always believed a mother would.

"Why don't you come out to meet your new family?"

Miss Switch held out a soft hand, which Margaret took as she climbed down from the car. Everything seemed to be happening in a blur.

"Children," said Miss Switch. "Say hello to your new sister, Margaret."

The fact that this beautiful woman knew her name was almost too much to take in, and Margaret barely heard as the children called out "Hello, Margaret!" in a chorus of voices.

As Miss Switch led her up the gleaming white steps and through the front door, it seemed to Margaret that she really was walking in a dream.

The house was warm and cozy, with comfy chairs and plush carpets and velvet drapes hanging from the windows. Miss Switch led Margaret into the dining room, where an enormous carved table was laid with silver platters of strawberries and cookies and tarts and cakes. It was more food than Margaret had seen in her entire life. She shivered with delight.

"Are you cold, dear?" Miss Switch asked.

Without waiting for an answer, she produced a delicate red shawl, which she draped over Margaret's shoulders. It was as soft as silk and the nicest piece of clothing Margaret had ever worn. When she breathed in, a delicious perfume filled her nose.

Hannah followed them inside and smiled when she saw the joy on Margaret's face. "I see everything here is still as lovely as I remember it," she said, looking at Miss Switch.

Miss Switch smiled, too, revealing two rows of even, pearly teeth.

"Of course, Hannah, dear. We were just about to sit down for tea." Turning from Hannah, she put a soft hand on Margaret's shoulder. "I hope you're hungry, sweetling."

Margaret nodded, wide-eyed, feeling she might burst into tears from so much happiness.

"Now then," said Gertrude, who had walked in with a purple clipboard. "Miss Switch, do you accept full responsibility for this pitiful foundling and hereby take guardianship of her from the C.L.C. from this point forward?"

"I do," said Miss Switch.

"And Marjorie," Gertrude said, reading from the

paper, "do you agree to this arrangement as well?"

"Yes!" breathed Margaret, barely louder than a whisper.

"Fine," said Gertrude, making checkmarks on the clipboard. "I'll just finish up this paperwork, and we'll be on our way."

"Are you sure you won't stay for tea, Gertrude?" said Miss Switch, turning from Margaret to the dining table.

"We shouldn't ... Procedure, you know," said Gertrude, reaching for a piece of poppyseed cake.

Margaret gazed out the window, where the red- and blue-clad children had begun a game of tag on the lawn. She had never seen so many children before, and her eyes darted from one to the other excitedly. As she watched, one pretty dark-haired girl ran past a smiling scrawny boy, smacking him hard across the back. A look of pain crossed the boy's face for a split second, but was quickly replaced by a new, even wider smile.

Margaret thought this seemed a little strange, but before she could glimpse any more —

"All done!" said Gertrude, wiping her mouth and snapping the clipboard shut.

"Such a pleasure, as always, ladies," Miss Switch said, ushering Gertrude out the door.

"It's time for us to go, Margaret," said Hannah, dropping to her knees. "Good luck," she whispered. "And call if you need anything."

"Thanks," said Margaret. "But I don't think I will."

Hannah pulled her into a gentle hug.

Bleeeeeeeep. The car horn blared outside, making

them both jump. Then with a last smile, Hannah ran to join the others.

Trailing behind, Margaret was just in time to see the shiny pink car start off down the road, raising a cloud of dust behind it. Miss Switch was waving a handkerchief, and Margaret stood beside her and waved, too.

"Goodbye!" she called out. "And thank you!"

She watched the dust settle on the road and hoped that soon she, too, would be settled.

Gone were thoughts of bossy old ladies, and crowded buses, and mysterious signs on quiet streets. From now on, this wonderful place would be her home, and these wonderful people, her family.

CHAPTER 5

PHILANTHROPY

At this happy and hopeful point in our tale, let us leave Margaret to enjoy herself for just a moment. Let us leave that important day and go back to one that came long before it.

If you have passed enough time in this world, you will have noticed that every great event is the result of many smaller things that happened before it. Had Cousin Amos put more stock in washing his socks, for instance, he might never have caught antisanitosis. Had Margaret not run out of parents and relatives to take care of her, she might never have come to the Hopeton Orphanage. And had a certain town meeting not taken place many years before that, the Hopeton Orphanage might never have come into existence at all.

"Order!" cried the Mayor to the townspeople, at this very meeting.

The young Mayor, who was called Harold Picklewort,

banged a small gavel against his podium. There was very little noise in the town hall, since the people of Hopeton prided themselves on manners, but Mayor Picklewort greatly enjoyed banging his gavel.

"Order!" he cried again, with three more bangs for good measure.

He cleared his throat loudly.

"We are here today to discuss *philanthropy*," he said, pausing to let the grandness of this word sink in.

"As you all know," he continued, "over in Munsfield, they've recently turned their general store into a soup kitchen."

Angry mutterings rose from the crowd.

"Yes," said the Mayor. "Once again, Munsfield is trying to show us up. Trying to make us look bad. Which is why we need to figure out what sort of philanthropy we're going to do in return. We can't let them get away with this."

The crowd of heads nodded in agreement.

True philanthropy is a wonderful thing. If you have ever reunited a baby with its lost teddy bear, or helped an old granny cross the road, or returned a missing wallet to its owner, then you have done a bit of philanthropy yourself — so long as you didn't take any money from the wallet, granny or baby. True philanthropy is doing something kind for someone else without giving the slightest bit of thought to yourself.

Unfortunately, true philanthropy is not quite what the Mayor had brought the Hopetoners together to discuss.

A woman in the front row raised her hand. "How about a homeless shelter?" she asked.

"Definitely not," said the Mayor. "The hobos might start sleeping in it. The last thing we want is a bunch of hobos mussing up our philanthropy."

Mutters of agreement came from around the room, and the woman in the front row sank down in her chair.

"Why don't we build a soup kitchen, too?" someone said. "An even bigger soup kitchen!"

The Mayor shook his head. "No, no. If we do that, the Munsfielders will just say we copied them. There's got to be some philanthropy we can do that will really make them squirm in their boots!"

The townspeople furrowed their brows and fell to thinking about squirming Munsfielders.

"What about something for children?" came a voice from the back of the hall.

The Mayor's face lit up. "Yes!" he shouted. "Something for children! Everybody likes children, don't they?"

"An orphanage!" cried a thin, birdlike woman with a long pointy nose. "Somewhere we can put all the stray ragamuffins nobody wants. And far away from here, so they won't hang around our nice town."

The room began to buzz with excitement.

"Bingo!" said the Mayor. "An orphanage is much more philanthropic than a stuffy kitchen! That'd show those soup-sniffing Munsfielders!"

"I quite agree," said a gravelly voice, and everyone

turned to look at an important-looking old gentleman with bushy eyebrows, whose name was Professor Thrumble.

Professor Thrumble was the most well-educated man in town, having spent many years reading long and serious books, and many more years putting the schoolchildren of Hopeton to sleep with long and serious lectures.

"An orphanage," said Professor Thrumble, "is the perfect place to educate the excess population. It will prepare them for useful roles in society, should they ever cease to be children."

"Indeed!" said the birdlike woman, pleased that someone so well educated had approved her idea. "As chairwoman of the Knitting Society," she said, "I will take charge of rounding up the orphans. I am very concerned for these pitiful foundlings."

"So am I," said a dumpy woman with large bulgy eyes. "Very concerned."

"Shush, Prudie," said the birdlike woman, who, if you hadn't guessed, was Gertrude.

"Allow me to say a few words," said the Professor, and several of his listeners got ready to take a short nap. He was known for making long and serious speeches to people whether they were children or not. On that particular day, he gave a speech on the dangers of uneducated orphans.

"In conclusion," he finished fifteen minutes later, "if you should need a noble mind to guide these stray youths, I shall be happy to offer my wisdom."

The Professor gave a deep bow, Gertrude burst into

applause, and Mayor Picklewort, who had dozed off, shook himself awake and gave several loud bangs of his gavel.

"It's settled then!" the Mayor shouted, waking up the rest of the hall. "Professor Thrumble will take the post of Master of the new orphanage."

And with the Mayor banging his gavel, the townspeople chose a site on the very edge of the town limits on which to build their orphanage.

"We'll build a place for misplaced infants!" they cheered.

"A home for homeless tots!"

"Ooo, I can't wait to see the looks on the Munsfielders' faces!"

After the meeting, the townspeople trundled back to their cozy houses, and most of them never thought of their philanthropy again, except to inform any Munsfielder who hadn't heard of it.

This meeting led to quite a lot of paperwork, which led to quite a lot of money from the town treasury, which went to Gertrude and Prudence and was then mostly forgotten. And a few years after that, on an unwanted plot of land on the very edge of the town, the Hopeton Orphanage opened its doors.

They were the very same doors, in fact, that opened many years later to Margaret Grey. The same doors that led her to a home filled with happy laughing children, piles of wonderful things to eat, and the beautiful, smiling Miss Switch.

CHAPTER 6

THE SWITCH

When last we saw Margaret Grey, she was waving good-bye to a pink car, watching the dust settle on a long dirt road and hoping great hopes about her new life.

Just at that moment, a firm hand gripped her shoulder, making her turn around. Miss Switch was towering over her, her eyes following the pink car as it disappeared over a hill.

"Come now, dear," Miss Switch said, placing her other hand on Margaret's back and pushing her into the house.

The rest of the children filed in behind them. Margaret smiled, hoping to make a good first impression, but no one smiled back.

"Would you like help laying out the tea?" she asked, having always been taught to be a helpful houseguest.

There were several moments of empty silence.

Margaret looked around, wondering if perhaps no one had heard her.

A change seemed to have come over the house, though Margaret couldn't quite put her finger on what it was. All around the entry hall, the other children were looking at her very strangely. One small mousy-looking girl shook her head solemnly from side to side, her eyes wide.

"Um," said Margaret. "Miss Switch?"

Miss Switch didn't answer. Instead she did a very odd thing. She reached into her apron pocket and pulled out a thin, golden whistle. She put the whistle in her mouth and blew.

Tweeeeeeeet!

At the sound, the entire house seemed to come alive.

The children scattered in all directions. They ran into the kitchen and the dining room and the entryway, grabbing and pulling at everything around them as they went. Within moments the silver trays of cookies and tarts had disappeared into boxes, which disappeared into the kitchen. The lovely plush carpets and velvet drapes were yanked from their places and rolled up into tight little bundles that were carried away. Large white sheets were draped over the soft chairs, and splintery wooden stools were set around the table instead.

And the orphans were changing, too. They were helping each other out of their bright coveralls to reveal shabby gray clothes that looked as if they had been made from potato sacks.

"Hey!" Margaret cried, for several children had surrounded her and were pulling away her new shawl.

It may be that you do not understand what was happening, and if that is the case, you know exactly how poor Margaret was feeling. Before her eyes, the orphanage was changing from a beautiful, warm home to a cold, dingy house.

And Miss Switch! Miss Switch, who only moments before had been wearing a tattered flower-print apron, had transformed. She had pulled off her apron and unbuttoned the plain gray dress to reveal a luxurious red silk one underneath. Children had come running down the stairs carrying jewelry — strands of pearls and glittering stones — which they were draping one after the other around Miss Switch's long neck.

And another change had taken place, an even more terrible change. Miss Switch's beautiful face, which moments before had been filled with tenderness and motherly affection, was now sinister and cold. Her smile had hardened and turned positively carnivorous.

Margaret stared at her in horror. "What's going on?"

Miss Switch looked down at her in a way that made Margaret feel very small indeed. "I am Matron here," she said with a sneer. "And you, dreg, will call me Miss Switch."

She snapped her long fingers, and a pretty blonde girl who looked about thirteen stepped forward.

The girl was smiling at Margaret, but it was not a warm smile of welcome. It was the type of smile a hyena might give a tasty mutton chop right before devouring it.

"Every morning, dreg," the girl said, "you will wake up at sunrise and make your bed. You will gather the laundry and sweep the floors, then you'll go to the kitchen and make breakfast for your superiors. After that, you get four minutes to eat your breakfast mush. Then you will scrub the bathtubs and polish the toilets."

The girl went on, listing chore after chore to be done, while Margaret looked around in shock. From the faces of the other children, she could see that they, too, were forced to pluck weeds and scrub floors and wash dishes every hour of the day.

She turned desperately to Miss Switch, who was admiring her own glittery reflection in a large mirror on the wall.

"Miss Switch," she said, reaching out to touch the Matron's dress. "Please, I don't understand —"

Miss Switch spun around, slapping Margaret's hand from her dress with a loud clap.

"You will do as I tell you," she said fiercely. "You're a worthless dreg. Nobody wants you. Nobody likes you. And if you don't do what I say, I'll throw you out of your bed in the middle of the night and you will be gobbled up by rabid raccoons."

Margaret cradled her hand, her eyes filling with tears from the slap.

But instead of apologizing, or kissing it better, or doing any of the things a mother should do, Miss Switch began to laugh. It was a cold, harsh sound, like the screeching of a crow. And with a last grin at Margaret's disbelieving face, she swept out of the room.

For you see, every story has a villain. And in case you hadn't guessed, the villain of this story is Miss Switch.

CHAPTER 7

THE HOME OF THE DREGS

On her first night at the Hopeton Orphanage, Margaret cried herself into a fitful sleep.

When she awoke the next morning in her lumpy bed, several moments passed before she remembered where she was. But when a scowling boy with chestnut curls appeared and shook her roughly by the shoulders, the events of the previous day came rushing back.

"Up, dreg!" he shouted. "Make your bed!"

Margaret blinked around at the rows of narrow beds and yawning orphans. Across the room, other children were being kicked and poked awake by the cruel-looking blonde girl who had given the orders the day before.

"Ouch!" Margaret cried.

The curly-haired boy had pinched her on the arm.

"What are you staring at? Move faster when you get an order!" he said.

Margaret hurried to straighten her flimsy sheets, and the boy stomped off to the next bed.

"The first few days are always the worst," said a hushed voice, and Margaret saw the wide-eyed mousy girl who had shaken her head so solemnly the day before.

Margaret was full of questions, but before she could whisper any of them to the mousy girl, a screeching voice filled the room.

"You worthless little runtworm!"

The bossy blonde girl was snarling at a tiny boy who was struggling to lift a large laundry basket.

"You're the most useless snizzler I've ever seen!" spat the girl.

Grabbing the basket from the tiny boy's hands and lifting it high in the air, she tipped it over his head. Rolls of grimy socks tumbled out in a wave until the boy was buried in a smelly pyramid, then the girl dropped the basket so that it landed with a thump on top of the heap. She threw her head back and laughed loudly. The curly-haired boy snickered.

"That's Lacey Walloper," the mousy girl whispered. "One of Switch's Pets. And the other's Christopher Thrashley. You'll have to watch out for them. My name's Judy. Just follow me and do what I do."

Turning to a hamper of dirty towels, Judy grabbed hold of one side and Margaret took the other.

"Judy," Margaret whispered as they made their way out of the room, "what happened yesterday?"

"The Switch," said Judy. "That's what we call her when she's not around. She gets charity money from those ladies for the orphanage, but she only uses it on herself. She has to make everything look good when they come to visit, but they always telephone beforehand, so she has time to put out all the nice things."

"Couldn't you tell someone?" Margaret asked. "Couldn't you call the police?"

Judy shook her head sadly. "Some kids have tried, but no one believes them. And the Switch can make things really terrible for anyone who gets in her way." Judy lowered her voice. "Once, Phoebe Frizzleton forgot to smile when the C.L.C. ladies asked how she was. Switch made her stand in the middle of a field during a lightning storm. Phoebe couldn't sleep for weeks after that. It's best to just keep your head down and try not to get noticed."

Margaret and Judy filed down the hallway behind other pairs of orphans and their hampers. Then, one by one, they emptied their loads down an enormous laundry chute. Turning away from the chute, Margaret noticed a new group of children who had come from a neighboring room to join Lacey and Christopher. They were laughing with each other, and many had smug looks on their faces.

Judy nudged her. "The rest of the Pets," she whispered.

"What's a Pet?" Margaret asked.

Just at that moment Lacey came stalking down the

line so Judy didn't get a chance to tell her. But as that dreadful day progressed, Margaret learned the answer for herself.

Miss Switch, it soon became clear, divided the orphans into two groups. The ones she found to be cute and adorable she called Pets, while all the others were dregs.

The Pets were Miss Switch's personal favorites, and it was their job to keep the dregs in line. It was also their job to brush the Matron's hair, paint her toenails or simply follow her around and admire her. She would say things like, "My hair is less shiny today than usual," to which the Pets would respond, "Oh, no, Miss Switch! You have the loveliest hair in the world," and so on.

In return she treated them a great deal better than the less attractive orphans, who were forced to chop and cook and scrub and scrape and wash and weed all day long.

Margaret, as you already know, had become a dreg, which meant that her life was now full of just such scrubbing and scraping and washing and weeding. She had begun what is called *a life of drudgery*, which is the most unpleasant kind of life to have.

On Margaret's second day in the orphanage, Miss Switch ordered her to chop onions into perfectly square-shaped pieces for her egg-white omelet. By the time Margaret finished, her eyes were stinging and watering so much that she dropped her bowl of breakfast mush on the floor and had nothing to eat at all.

On Margaret's third day, Miss Switch put her on porch-scrubbing duty with a pimply-faced dreg called Bessie Blotchly. Margaret's hands got so sore from the scrub brush that painful blisters blossomed across her palms, and when she asked for permission to stop, Lacey gave her a row of hard pinches on her arm.

The day after that, Miss Switch discovered that a nervous dreg called Vickram Skitter had accidentally thrown away her new fashion magazines. As punishment, she threw him down the laundry chute with a rope tied around his waist, where he spent the afternoon whimpering quietly until Margaret and the others were allowed to haul him up again.

On the fifth day, Miss Switch commanded Margaret and the very smallest dreg, a puny boy called Timothy Smealing, to climb up into the chimney and scrape it out with toothbrushes. They got soot so far up their ears and noses that they couldn't hear or smell anything for the rest of the day, and Miss Switch sent them to bed without supper for having dirty fingernails.

As it happened, a young couple came to the orphanage that evening looking to adopt an orphan. But Margaret, lying in her bed with soot-filled ears and an empty stomach, didn't even get to lay eyes on them, and they took home a fetching black-haired Pet named Charlotte Ravenhurst.

Young as she was, Margaret had already faced a great number of unpleasant things. She had accepted her life of silence with Cousin Amos. She had endured Great-aunt Linda's bossiness. She had minded her manners and tried to make the best of things, and she had always obeyed the rules because that is what she had been taught to do.

But Margaret could see that Miss Switch was an entirely different kind of awful. Miss Switch wasn't going to guard her, or care for her, or help her in any way. For the first time, Margaret had fallen under the thumb of a truly cruel person.

Dealing with cruelty is a pretty tall order, even for grown-ups. But Margaret remembered what Hannah had whispered before driving away. *Call if you need anything.*

Margaret certainly needed something now. So, unused to boldness though she was, she concocted a very bold plan. And as she went about her chores, she waited patiently for a chance to act on it.

CHAPTER 8

THE TRUTH ABOUT BULLIES

Bullies, whether big or small, are really very much alike.

No matter how much they poke or pinch or tease, they never seem satisfied, which is a pity for whoever is being poked and pinched. The truth about bullies is that every one of them has a sore spot that pokes and pinches at *them*, like a bad stomachache or a pesky thorn stuck in their side. The sore spot might be caused by loneliness, or jealousy, or even fear, but every single bully has one, and it never goes away no matter how much bullying they do.

Miss Switch, who was one of the biggest bullies of all, was no different. Though she brought orphan after terrified orphan to the brink of despair, she never seemed satisfied, and the sore spot never went away. For the thorn sticking in Miss Switch's side was *beauty*.

Though anyone would say that the Matron was beautiful now, she knew she had once been much more than that. Not so many years ago, she had been breathtaking — the type of person you would stop and stare at if you saw her walking down the street.

One day when she was quite young, two people had stopped to stare at her who were very important indeed.

"Rolph! Do you see zat girl?" one of them said, a woman with dark sunglasses and tall spiky heels.

"Oh my, yes!" said Rolph, who wore a long ponytail. "Dah-ling!"

"Excusez-moi!" cried the woman, waving a silk handkerchief at Miss Switch. "Mademoiselle, a moment!"

And they swooped down on the young Miss Switch like hungry bees on a flower.

" 'Ave you ever posed for a portrait?" asked the woman.

"Dah-ling, what a face!" cried Rolph.

Young Miss Switch, who was unused to this sort of attention, had a feeling that a wonderful new life was about to start for her.

As it turned out, the spiky-heeled woman was called Estella Isabella, and she owned a very successful fashion magazine. Rolph, who had no last name, was a world-famous photographer. They both found Miss Switch to be so lovely that from that point on, her only job was to sit for portraits.

In the grand scheme of things, sitting for portraits is neither a useful nor an interesting job. But Miss Switch didn't mind. She made a large group of stylish new friends and bought all the best clothing and jewelry to adorn herself with. Each day seemed better and more glamorous than the last, and she truly believed that she could very happily spend the rest of her life in the world of fashion.

In that world, you see, people with beautiful faces have a lot of control over those around them. And Miss Switch, with the most beautiful face of all, controlled a great many people.

She controlled the man who painted on her makeup and the seamstresses who hemmed her gowns. She controlled the girl who brought her lunch and the woman who cleaned her dressing room. If she didn't like the way things were done, she could pout and hold up everyone's day until she got her way. Her portraits were so important to everyone that no one dared refuse her anything.

But the one thing Switch couldn't control was time.

Years passed, and her shiny hair became the tiniest bit duller. Her skin became just a smidgen less glowing. And one fateful day, just as Switch was about to have her portrait taken with an enormous peacock, the makeup man screamed and dropped his brush.

"What is it?" said Miss Switch in alarm, for he looked as though he'd seen something really dreadful.

"Nothing to worry about!" said the man. "I'll just need some more powder."

But when Miss Switch checked her reflection in the mirror, she saw what had made the makeup man scream. Right in the middle of her smooth forehead was a tiny wrinkle.

That was the last photograph ever taken of Miss Switch. Rolph stopped asking her for portraits, and Estella wouldn't return her phone calls.

Switch lingered near the fashionable shops and restaurants in the hope of bumping into them, but all the waiters and shopkeepers who had once been so happy to see her now seemed to turn their heads away. At last she spotted the pair of them at a sidewalk café, sitting next to a tall willowy girl with black hair.

"Rolph!" Switch cried. "Estella!" But neither of them showed any interest at all.

"What do *you* want?" asked Estella.

"You haven't been returning my messages," Switch said.

"Dah-ling," said Rolph. "You're *out.*"

"What?" said Switch. "What do you mean?"

"You're finished," Rolph said. "Kaput. Zippo. No one wants you."

Although this was an awful thing for Rolph to say, and Miss Switch felt as though she'd been struck by lightning, she turned hopefully to Estella. "Couldn't I at least work at your magazine?" she asked.

"Why should we want *you*," Estella said, sticking up her nose, "when zere are so many ozzer girls who are so much more beautiful? So much younger. No, I don't see zat we vill 'ave any use for you."

"Then," Switch said quietly, "what am I to do?"

"I'm afraid you vill just 'ave to go and join ze dregs of society," said Estella with a cold smile. Then she turned back to the willowy girl beside her. "Now, if you vill excuse us, we are getting to know more about Chi-Chi 'ere."

"You're going to be a star, dah-ling," Rolph said to the willowy girl, already ignoring the devastated Miss Switch.

From that moment on, it was as if a door had closed on Miss Switch, and she was never to be allowed back through. Her fancy friends would no longer speak to her. She couldn't afford the extravagant clothes and jewels she had grown used to. Every part of the world she had loved quickly slipped away.

The only thing her old life had given her was a lot of practice at ordering people around. Which is why, when she read about the retirement of the Master of Hopeton Orphanage in the newspaper, she applied to replace him.

"I think this job will be just right for you," said the cheerful young woman named Hannah Tender as she drove Miss Switch to the orphanage. "I'm sure you'll liven the place right up."

But Miss Switch soon found that the job was *not* right for her. With every passing day she grew more bitter, and her heart grew colder. Every time she noticed a new wrinkle on her creamy skin, she felt fury bubble up inside her like a smoldering volcano. And the children, who seemed to her a constant reminder of her own lost youth, were what she hated most of all.

By the time Margaret arrived at the orphanage, wide-eyed and hopeful, it seemed to Switch as though every child was a pin stuck in her side, poking and pricking and needling her by their very presence. It was only when she crushed the spirit right out of the children that she felt a moment's ease. But no matter how terrible Switch made life in the orphanage, it was never terrible enough.

CHAPTER 9

TEASPOONS AND TREACHERY

At the end of Margaret's first week, Miss Switch ordered her to polish all the silverware in the scullery, which was a small room behind the kitchen. The Pet assigned to guard her was a girl called Agatha Spink.

Agatha had shining dark hair that fell almost to her waist, a rather bulbous nose and, as it happened, a very short attention span. This turned out to be a lucky thing for Margaret, because the only thing duller than polishing silverware is keeping watch over someone else who is polishing silverware.

As Margaret polished the teaspoons, Agatha sighed and tapped her foot. As Margaret polished the dessert forks, Agatha rapped her fingers on the scullery door. And as the hours passed, Agatha twitched and fidgeted and wriggled and squirmed.

"Listen, dreg!" she said at last. "Don't even think of

doing anything funny. If you're not finished by the time I get back, I'll put pepper in your mush for a week."

"Yes, Agatha," Margaret said, giving her a fearful, obedient look.

Agatha narrowed her eyes like a rat, then stepped aside and let the scullery door swing shut with Margaret inside.

As soon as she was gone, Margaret dropped to the ground. Through the crack under the door, she saw the dark-haired Pet disappearing into the pantry where all the cookies and treats were kept.

And in that moment, Margaret knew her chance had come. For the first time since arriving at the orphanage, she knew that no one was watching her. For the first time, she was alone.

Sneaking around in places you don't belong is called trespassing, and it is usually a very rude thing to do. Imagine, for example, jumping into your bed one night and finding a strange banker tucked up under the covers. Not only would you have to discuss economics as you shooed the banker outside, but you would probably find that he had arranged your pillows in exactly the wrong way. No one enjoys having a stranger puttering about uninvited, which is why trespassing is such an impolite habit.

But after a week at the Hopeton Orphanage, Margaret knew that a stint of impoliteness would be the least of her problems.

As quietly as she could, Margaret pushed the scullery door open and slipped through it. She listened to Agatha munching away on cookies for a few seconds, then tiptoed out of the kitchen and into the hallway.

Along with Switch's bedroom, her sitting room and her private bathroom, Switch's study was right up there with the den of a hungry lion as one of the worst places on earth to go trespassing. But this is just where Margaret was headed. Because even though the study was off limits, it had the one thing she needed more than anything: a telephone.

The Matron's study was at the far end of the hallway, and when Margaret reached the door, she put her ear against the keyhole to check if any Pets were inside. There wasn't a peep, so she turned the handle and crept through the door.

The room inside was a cozy one, lined with book-shelves and marble sculptures of famous people's heads. The first Master of Hopeton had stacked the shelves with leather-bound books, but Switch had filled them with her enormous collection of glossy fashion magazines instead.

Ignoring both the magazines and the marble heads, Margaret made straight for the telephone on the wide oak desk. With shaking hands, she picked up the receiver and dialed.

"Operator," said a nasal voice on the other end of the line.

"Concerned Ladies' Club, please," breathed Margaret, afraid to speak too loudly.

"Thank you," said the operator. There were three beeps on the other end of the line, then silence.

"Hello?" said a sweet voice at last, and Margaret felt a surge of hope. It was Hannah.

"Hannah! It's Margaret! Do you remember me?"

"Of course I remember you, Margaret. What's wrong?"

"Please come quickly and bring the police!" Margaret whispered. "It's all a fraud. All the furniture and the food and the clothes — Miss Switch put it all away as soon as you left. She uses the money for herself. We aren't looked after at all, we're worked all day long and —"

"What?" interrupted Hannah. "Margaret, is this true?"

"Yes. Oh, Hannah, please come!"

"I'll be there as fast as I can."

"Oh, thank you! I —" Margaret froze. For a moment, she thought she had heard a small noise outside the study door.

"I have to go!" she said in a rush, and hung up the phone.

Trembling, she crossed back to the door and peered through the keyhole. There was no one there.

Weak with relief, Margaret slipped back to the scullery. And as she sat, polishing away at the soup-spoons, wonderful thoughts began swimming through her mind.

Soon Hannah would come to the rescue, and all the orphans would be freed from their lives of drudgery and, best of all, they would never have to lay eyes on Miss Switch again.

All this would no doubt have happened, had it not been for one thing that poor Margaret knew nothing about.

CHAPTER 10

THE DREGGISH PET

As you know, the Matron of the Hopeton Orphanage had a habit of dividing her orphans into two groups based on their looks. What you may not know is that she always acted on first impressions.

This meant that if you arrived at the orphanage with messy hair and dark circles under your eyes from traveling, Miss Switch would sneer and shove a broom into your hands. It didn't matter if days or years afterwards you became a great beauty. "Once a dreg, always a dreg," was one of Miss Switch's favorite sayings.

The girl named Agatha Spink had arrived on the orphanage steps only a few weeks before Margaret on what happened to be a beautiful and sunny afternoon. The first time Miss Switch laid eyes on the new arrival, warm sunlight was bouncing off her lovely dark hair, so the Matron's first impression was one of shining raven locks that tumbled over the girl's shoulders in a very becoming way. Naturally, Switch smiled and offered her a strawberry tart.

It was not until the following morning that Miss Switch got a good look at the girl's large and bulbous nose.

"Who are you?" Switch snapped when Agatha brought in a jug of cucumber water.

"I'm Agatha Spink," Agatha replied, suddenly nervous.

Miss Switch stared at the girl in confusion. Then her look changed to one of disgust, and Agatha felt her knees buckle. Disgust was a look the Matron gave only to dregs.

"Go," Switch said, snatching the jug from her hands. "Send in someone else to help me dress. Send in one of the others."

As she scurried from the room, Agatha realized the mistake that had been made. She oughtn't to have been a Pet at all.

From that moment on, Agatha wasn't allowed in the Matron's private rooms, but neither could Miss Switch assign her to chores. The Matron's decisions in these matters were always final, and to admit that she'd made a mistake would be unthinkable. Instead, Agatha was given the least desirable of the Pets' tasks.

"Miss Switch really ought to just boot her out," Agatha overheard Lacey telling the other Pets one day. "She can't stand the sight of her — she's so *dreggish*. I'm telling you, one of these days we'll wake up and that big schnoz will be gone. Miss Switch'll see to that."

Agatha tried her very best to get back on Switch's

good side, but this only seemed to make the Matron more annoyed. As time went on, Agatha grew more and more certain that her days in the orphanage were numbered.

On the day of the silverware polishing, as she stood in the scullery watching Margaret shining spoon after spoon, these were the thoughts going round in Agatha's head.

What was the point, she asked herself, of doing what she was told, if she was going to be booted out no matter how hard she tried? She might as well enjoy herself while she still had a place to sleep at night.

Having reached this conclusion, she left Margaret and the silverware, dashed over to the pantry and began stuffing her mouth with cookies.

Desperate people, you see, will often try to distract themselves from their worries. Some of the dregs threw themselves into their chores until they could no longer think clearly. Others tried to convince themselves that they were in the middle of a long and unpleasant dream from which they would soon wake up. Unfortunately, neither of these strategies could keep their troubles at bay for long. And as satisfying as it was to stuff her mouth with sugary treats, Agatha's method was no better.

After a few minutes in the pantry, Agatha's stomach was pleasantly full, but her worries were as real as ever. Wiping the crumbs from her mouth, she shuffled back to the scullery to check on Margaret …

And you already know what she discovered. The polishing had been abandoned, and the little brown-haired dreg had disappeared.

Agatha's knees began to shake. Pet or not, a slip-up like this would be the last straw for her.

Which is why, in a sudden panic, she took off down the hall to search for the missing girl. It is also why, when she overheard the dreg's telephone call through the very same keyhole Margaret had peered through only moments before, she ran immediately to Miss Switch and told her every word of it.

Surely, thought Agatha, warning Miss Switch of such a plot would bring her back into the Matron's good graces.

And when Miss Switch, who hated the very sight of the big-nosed child gasping in her doorway, heard what the girl had to say, she smiled a very sinister smile indeed.

CHAPTER II

NOTHING WORSE
THAN A THIEF

Margaret had been polishing for what felt like a very long time. She was just beginning to wonder how much longer the raven-haired Pet would stay in the pantry when she heard the sound of approaching footsteps. She started polishing a little faster just in case the Pet was in a scolding mood, but it wasn't Agatha who pulled open the door.

It was Miss Switch, wearing a turquoise satin dressing gown.

The Matron stared down at Margaret with a look of pure sweetness, her golden hair shining. "It's Margaret, isn't it?" she said, and her voice reminded Margaret of a purring cat.

"Yes, Miss Switch," said Margaret, who was beginning to have a very bad feeling in the pit of her stomach.

"My," purred Miss Switch, "what a nice job you've done with the polishing."

"Thank you," said Margaret.

"Why don't you take a little break?" Stepping to one side, Miss Switch swept her arm in a wide gesture to the kitchen, and Margaret, not knowing what else to do, stepped slowly forward.

Glancing around, she saw that Lacey was standing near the hallway door, smiling the hyena-like smile that made Margaret feel more like a lamb chop than a little girl.

"Perhaps," Miss Switch said softly, "you wouldn't mind helping Lacey fetch my silk scarf from upstairs? I have a bit of a chill."

Margaret frowned slightly, certain the Matron would never ask a dreg to perform such a personal task. But she took a deep breath and said, "No, I wouldn't mind."

"Marvelous," said Miss Switch.

"Follow me," said Lacey.

Margaret followed her up the stairs. When they reached the top, Lacey led the way to a large closet and pulled open the door.

"It's in here," Lacey said. "Near the back. Go on."

Margaret hesitated. She knew there was a good chance Lacey was up to something, and a very good chance it was something cruel. But she also knew that help couldn't be far away, and that she need only play along until it arrived. So, with a nod, she stepped into the closet.

Not surprisingly, the door slammed shut behind her and locked with a click. But what was surprising was the sound that echoed through the house only seconds later.

Tweeeeeeeeet!

The whistle!

"No!" Margaret cried, banging on the closet door. Now she knew what was happening. The only possible thing that could ruin her hopes of rescue: Miss Switch had ordered the switch once again. Even now, the orphans were covering the house in fine things and changing into their colorful coveralls and hiding all evidence of Miss Switch's treachery.

"Stop!" cried Margaret. "Don't do it!"

But it was no use. Soon the commotion had stopped, and Margaret knew that the truth had been hidden once again. A few minutes passed, and then she heard the sounds of a car approaching and a hard knock at the front door.

"Good evening, Miss Switch." A man's voice drifted up from the entryway.

"Sheriff, how nice to see you," came Miss Switch's voice at its most charming. "I do hope all is well? Hello, ladies."

"I'm dreadfully sorry about the disturbance," came Gertrude's sharp voice, sounding annoyed. "This is completely against procedure."

"Yes, indeed," said Prudie's voice. "We never visit without calling ahead. It's impolite."

But then Hannah spoke, and Margaret felt a surge of hope.

"I'm afraid I've just had a telephone call from one of your children," Hannah said. "She told me some very disturbing things about — about the way you run things here ..." Hannah's voice trailed off.

Margaret knew she was looking around at all the beautiful things that Margaret had insisted wouldn't be there.

"How very odd," said Miss Switch.

"Everything looks fine to me," said the Sheriff.

"And me," said Gertrude.

"Yes," said Hannah. "But where is Margaret? I'd like to speak with her."

"By all means. Margaret!" Miss Switch called in a singsong voice.

On cue, the key turned in the lock and Lacey pulled Margaret from the closet. She shoved her toward the stairs with a smirk.

Worrying about possible punishment as you climb a flight of stairs is an unpleasant feeling. *Knowing* that your doom awaits you at the bottom of one is even worse.

But Margaret had no choice. As she came down the stairs, she saw that the floorboards were now richly carpeted. She saw the orphans in their bright clothes and Miss Switch in a faded gingham sundress. She saw the remains of a delicious-looking lunch spread out on the table. She saw Hannah's kind face, looking confused, and the Concerned Ladies, looking miffed, and a mustachioed man in uniform who must be the Sheriff.

"Oh!" said Miss Switch. "What were you doing up

there, Margaret? And in your painting frock? I thought you'd be playing in the yard with the others."

"Yes," said Gertrude. "From noon until one-thirty, the children play out of doors. It's in the schedule."

Margaret turned to Hannah and opened her mouth to explain, but before she could get even a single word out —

"Miss Switch!" Lacey bellowed from the top of the stairs. "Margaret has been *stealing* from you!"

At these words, five gasps sounded — four genuine ones from the ladies and the Sheriff and a theatrical one from Miss Switch. Lacey rushed downstairs, and handed something to the Matron. "I found this in that ratty bag under her bed."

"I can't believe it!" As though she were on a stage, Miss Switch held up a beautiful pearl necklace. "This is a treasured family heirloom!"

"Well it certainly doesn't belong under a child's bed then," said Prudie. "Jewelry belongs in a jewelry case."

"Marjorie must have taken it!" cried Gertrude. "It's the only logical explanation."

"There's nothing worse than a thief," said the Sheriff, looking stern.

Hannah looked at Margaret very closely, a mixture of surprise and confusion on her face. "I don't understand," she said. "Margaret, did you do this?"

Margaret shook her head frantically, then opened her mouth to defend herself.

"Margaret, how could you?" Miss Switch cut in loudly,

bringing her hand to her forehead and turning back to the group. Hannah was staring at Miss Switch now with a slight frown on her face.

"I'm so sorry you had to see this, Sheriff," Miss Switch went on. "I'm afraid the child must be starved for attention to be acting out like this. It's a matter for a mother's gentle touch, not the firm hand of the law."

"Well, all right," said the Sheriff. "I must say you're being very forgiving about the whole thing. And you," he added sternly, turning to Margaret. "If I hear you're giving Miss Switch any more trouble, I can tell you that I won't be nearly so understanding."

"Nor will we," said Prudie, her plump face pink with annoyance.

"Please accept our apologies, Miss Switch," said Gertrude. "If we'd known this child had criminal tendencies, we'd have sent her straight to the loony bin."

"You can always tell the bad ones," added Prudie, "because they're less adorable than the others. That is something I know to be absolutely true."

"It's not!" Margaret finally managed to say, but no one was listening. Already Switch was ushering them all out to the porch and down the front steps. Only Hannah turned to look back before she climbed into the police car with the others and they set off down the dirt road.

Margaret looked wildly around at the other orphans, but none of them would even look at her.

It was over. Margaret had failed. And Switch, the horrible, beautiful Switch, had most definitely won.

PART TWO

THE MOTHS

CHAPTER 12

THE DREG WHO DIDN'T EXIST

When the mousy girl called Judy told Margaret to keep her head down and try not to get noticed, it was for a very good reason. Drawing attention to yourself when Miss Switch was around, whether through a tiny hint of cheekiness or a grand act of rebellion, meant you were in for punishment.

"So," said Switch in her purring voice when she returned from the porch. "You like to blab, do you? You like to chit-chat with policemen?" Her glittering eyes pierced Margaret's, and the corners of her mouth turned slowly up. "Well, blabby dregs must learn to shut their mouths."

She turned to the other orphans.

"Those are the last words anyone is to speak to this dreg," she said coolly. "If any of you so much as whisper to her, I'll tape your mouth shut for a month."

"Yes, Miss Switch," said the orphans.

"And you," she turned to Margaret, "had best not make another sound for the rest of your pitiful life, or I'll feed you to a pack of coyotes."

Miss Switch unplugged the telephone and locked it away in her bedroom. And from that day on, the others acted as if Margaret wasn't there.

She was made to do her chores completely on her own. Instead of screaming their orders at her in the usual way, the Pets would silently swat her on the head, shove a rag or broom at her and point in the direction she was to go. Her bed was moved out of the dregs' room into the hallway, where it caught a very chilly draft. And at mealtimes her food was put out on the porch, where she had to sit and eat it all alone.

Through it all, no one spoke a single word to her, not even Judy. To add injury to insult, the Pets gave her extra pinches to make up for their usual name calling.

It is a very unpleasant thing, being treated like you don't exist. A person with a weaker disposition than Margaret might think that they'd turned invisible without noticing, and would have to check a mirror every five minutes to be sure they were still there.

Margaret, though, kept her wits about her. No matter how much she was pinched and poked and prodded, she was careful never to make the slightest peep. In fact, after going a full day without saying a word to anyone, she was beginning to think she could bear her punishment quite well.

On Margaret's second day of silence, however, word

went round that the Hopeton Orphanage was to receive two very special visitors: *parents*.

The arrival of potential parents at the orphanage was always a momentous occasion, because the thought of parents awakened a flutter of hope in every orphan. Unfortunately for the dregs, this hope was short-lived.

Every time a new couple came calling, Miss Switch would arrange the orphans in neat rows in the front hall, placing all of her most charming Pets in the very front. That way, they were the first ones the visitors saw when they stepped into the room.

She would coach the Pets on how to smile in the most adorable way and to give proper bows and curtseys. Then, at the back of the room, she would arrange the dregs.

"They'd have to be dotty to look at any of you," Switch would say with a glare. "But if they do, don't even think about saying something stupid. I can promise that you'll regret it later."

On this particular day, as the orphans stood in their rows wearing their red and blue coveralls, Margaret was tucked away in the very farthest corner of the room behind lanky Phoebe Frizzleton, whose poufy hair was blocking Margaret's face.

As the sound of a car engine came drifting through the window, Miss Switch appeared in a plain brown dress and a frilly white apron and made one final inspection of the Pets in the front row. Peering around Phoebe's shoulder, Margaret could see the curly-haired boy called Christopher Thrashley standing front and center, with Lacey at his side.

Switch disappeared from the room, and a few moments later she returned with a sweet-looking woman in a polka-dot dress and a man with a neat mustache.

"These are the orphans," Miss Switch said with a sweep of her arm, as she led the couple before the waiting children.

"Oh!" cried the woman, whose eyes immediately fell on Christopher Thrashley.

"Indeed," said the man, who looked as though he thought this fact was rather obvious.

"Please take your time," said Miss Switch. "And feel free to ask me any questions. I have the personal histories of each child available should you wish to read them."

The couple walked slowly along the first row of children before the sweet-faced woman came to a stop in front of Christopher.

"Hello, dear," she said. "What's your name?"

"I'm Christopher," he said, with a charming little bow. "It's very lovely to meet you!"

The woman beamed with delight and cast a quick glance at her husband, who nodded approvingly.

Beneath their smiles, the other orphans breathed a sigh of disappointment.

But just at that moment, an unexpected thing happened. Phoebe Frizzleton's poufy hair, which had been hanging down in front of Margaret's face, tickled her nose in precisely the wrong way, and Margaret gave a very loud, very high-pitched sneeze.

Every face in the room, including those of the man and woman, turned to look at Margaret, who clapped both of her hands over her mouth.

"Bless you, child!" said the woman, sweetly. "Martin, your hankie."

The man pulled a white handkerchief from his jacket pocket and edged between the rows of children to offer it to Margaret. "Here you are, little girl."

With a small curtsy, Margaret took it.

"And what might your name be?" asked the man.

Margaret opened her mouth to answer, but just at that moment, she caught a glimpse of Miss Switch. The Matron was standing behind the man and the woman, just out of sight so that neither of them could see her. And her face was wearing an expression so frightening that Margaret didn't dare utter a single sound.

She froze, looking up at the friendly man with her mouth half open, then pressed her lips tightly together and dropped her eyes to the floor.

"That child," Miss Switch said in a mock whisper, the sweetness in her face restored, "has a history of loopiness, I'm afraid. Runs in the family. It's best not to upset her."

"Oh!" said the man, staring at Margaret in shock and backing away quickly.

"Well, what about this one, Miss Switch?" asked the woman, pointing back to Christopher Thrashley.

Miss Switch smiled. "Christopher is one of our most

popular and well-behaved children. You won't find a more adorable child anywhere, I assure you."

At a final nod from the friendly man, the sweet-faced woman smiled with delight. "We'll take him!" she said.

But Margaret barely heard what happened next. As Christopher whooped and ran into the arms of his new parents, all Margaret could hear were the words she wished she could have said to the friendly man and woman.

"My name is Margaret Grey," she would have said. "I'm not loopy, it's just that I can't make a sound or I'll be fed to the coyotes. Please take me far away from here."

But of course, the man and the woman couldn't read minds.

The papers were signed. And as the new family said their goodbyes and climbed into their car and drove away down the dirt road, Margaret stared intently downwards, her eyes blurry with tears.

CHAPTER 13

SERENDIPITY

Margaret's Great-aunt Linda had often said, "If life gives you lemons, make lemonade," which was her way of saying that you should try to make the best of a bad situation. However, a far more useful saying would be, "If life gives you lemons, water, sugar, a pitcher and a long spoon to stir with, make lemonade." Everyone knows that if life gives you lemons alone it is just bad luck, and the most you can do is try to trade them for something better.

But if life gives you lemons and you are already in possession of water, sugar, a pitcher and a long spoon to stir with, that is something else entirely. That is *serendipity*.

Margaret Grey had lived in silence once before. And because she had once lived in silence, her new punishment — though she didn't realize it yet — was a stroke of serendipity.

Even though she was very lonesome without anyone to speak to, and even though her arms became bruised and sore from all the pinches, Margaret found that the quiet was strangely familiar. As day after day went by without even a hint of conversation, she began to notice a very odd thing.

The first time it happened, she was dusting the kitchen rafters from the top of a teetering ladder. As she swept her duster across a cobwebby beam, sending a great cloud of dust into the air, she heard —

Achoo!

Margaret nearly fell off her ladder, because for a split second, she thought she'd heard a sneeze coming from a spider's web.

That's ridiculous, she told herself, giving her head a shake. No one can hear a spider sneeze.

But a few days later, it happened again. She was sweeping under the kitchen table, cleaning up after Miss Switch's afternoon feast, when from somewhere in the walls —

Grumble.

Margaret bumped her head on the underside of the table. She could have sworn she'd heard the growl of a tiny mousy stomach.

That's absurd, she reminded herself, rubbing her sore head. No one can hear a mouse's hungry belly.

But with every passing day, it happened more and more.

She would be scrubbing the front steps and hear a

crow land on the roof. She would be cleaning the Pets' bedroom upstairs and hear two dregs whispering all the way down in the basement.

Margaret knew these events were ridiculous. She knew they were absurd. She knew that, in a sensible world, they simply couldn't be. But just because something is absurd or ridiculous doesn't stop it from being true. And as the very smallest of sounds continued to trickle in, she realized what was happening.

She was hearing things no one else could hear.

Without even noticing she was doing it, Margaret had started to *listen* again. You see, there are some talents that can never really be lost. They are only hiding, like a sleeping turtle in its shell, waiting to be coaxed out and used again.

As Margaret went mutely about her tasks, she soon discovered something else: she could control her talent. When she focused all her attention on her ears, she felt them *open* to the faintest and tiniest hints of sound.

At first it was only by closing her eyes and holding very still that she was able to do it perfectly. But late at night when everyone else was asleep, she practiced, and soon even with her eyes open or her hands busy at chores, she could focus her ears as easily as anything.

And the more she focused, the more she heard.

One evening, just as dusk was falling, Margaret was kneeling in the vegetable patch in the yard behind the orphanage. But rather than feeling lonesome and sad as she yanked spiky weeds from the rows of tomato plants, she was focusing her attention on her ears.

A hummingbird hovered nearby, and she heard each whir of its tiny wings.

A mole crawled by under the ground, and she heard its breath puff in and out.

A breeze blew across a clump of dandelions, and she heard each fluffy seed break off and float away on the wind.

"Wake up!" cried a very small voice.

Margaret looked up in surprise, wondering who had spoken, but no one was there.

"Come on, Pip, or we'll start without you!" cried the voice.

Margaret got to her feet and whirled around.

At the back of the vegetable patch was a trellis fence grown over with snap peas, and it was from this direction that the voice had come.

There was nothing behind the trellis, Margaret knew. Only a stretch of overgrown grass and the row of bushes that marked the end of the orphanage grounds. Unlike the front of the property, which was kept neatly trimmed and pruned to impress visitors, this part of the yard wasn't tended at all, since no one ever bothered to go there.

Margaret peered through a gap in the trellis, and sure enough, there wasn't a soul in sight.

"I'm coming!" called a new tiny voice.

"Hello?" cried Margaret. The voice sounded as though it must be right in front of her. "Who's there?"

But in that moment, Margaret had lost her focus, and her ears had closed up again as though someone had snapped a pair of earmuffs over them. Listen as she might, she didn't hear the mysterious voices again.

CHAPTER 14

THE THORNY BRUSH

Later that night, after Margaret had finished her chores and collapsed in her chilly bed in the hallway, she could think of nothing but the two strange voices.

The only people who could hear voices from nowhere, she had been brought up to believe, were people who'd gone a bit dotty in the head. But Margaret didn't feel any more dotty than usual. And as she lay there, tossing and turning in the cold, she realized something.

Quite accidentally, Miss Switch had given her an opportunity.

Now that her bed was separate from the others, there was no one around to see her come and go. There was no creaking bedroom door to alert the Pets. And there was no reason she could think of not to return to the yard to seek out the voices once again.

As everyone else lay sleeping, Margaret threw off her covers and laced up her shoes. She tiptoed from her bed and crept down the hallway, past the Pets' door and down the stairs. She crept through the kitchen and, very quietly, let herself out through the back door. Then she waited, wondering if anyone would come chasing after her to snatch her back inside. When no one did, she ran out into the moonlit yard.

Margaret ran through the garden, passing patches of carrots and turnips, all the way to the trellis fence with its trailing pea vines. But this time, she went around it. When she came to the other side, she felt her heart beat a little faster.

She was standing on the overgrown lawn on the other side of the trellis. Before her, a cool wind was blowing through the tall grass, and at the far end of the lawn, a tangle of bushes rose up in shadow.

"Hello?" she called, walking slowly forward.

All she could hear was the wind in the grass.

The bushes were gray in the moonlight, twisted and thorny and rather frightening. They had been left to grow wild for so long that they had joined together into a brush, too thick to see through and too tall to see over, with sharp branches that swayed in the wind as if clawing at the air.

Margaret came to the center of the lawn and stopped. She shivered, gazing up at the looming brush, then closed her eyes to calm her nerves. And it was then, with the swaying grass tickling her legs and the wind rustling her hair, that she heard the strange voices for the second time.

"Is it still there?" said a small voice. "What's it doing?"

"Just standing around," said another.

Margaret's eyes snapped open. Just as before, there was no one in sight, but she was sure this time — the voices had come from the enormous brush.

She took a step closer. As she did, she saw that in the bottom branches in the very center of the tangled brush, there was a gap.

The gap wasn't very large or very noticeable, but when she crouched down, she saw that it was just big enough for a raccoon or a fox or, perhaps, a very small girl. She pushed aside one thorny branch, then another, and soon the gap had widened enough for her to squeeze through it.

Slowly, Margaret reached her hand inside. Her hand was shortly followed by her wrist. Then her elbow, her shoulder, and finally her head. Carefully clearing a way through the brush, Margaret crawled deeper in. Then, quite suddenly, the branches gave way to open space, and Margaret looked up with a gasp.

The dense brush had been hiding something. At the heart of the growth of bushes, there was a tree.

The tree had a wrinkly, moss-covered trunk and a thick net of intertwined branches that fell all the way down to the ground. Margaret blinked several times, getting used to the dimness, and saw that she was in a sort of hollow that had formed between the branches and the trunk. When she breathed in, she inhaled a rich, mossy smell.

It was so lovely that she forgot to be puzzled. She forgot all about being dotty in the head. Gazing around at the beautiful, hidden chamber in the tree, Margaret listened.

She heard the call of a distant bird, and the soft breathing of the sleeping children in the orphanage.

She heard the parting of two clouds far overhead, and the dust blowing out on the road.

And when she concentrated very hard, she could even hear the leaves growing on the tree.

"Stay very still, Pipperflit," said a small voice. "Maybe it'll leave."

"No, Pip, fly away!" said another tiny voice. "It looks like a gobbler!"

Margaret looked down and saw a small shadowy creature sitting on a low branch near her right hand.

It was a moth.

CHAPTER 15

THE MOTH TREE

"What's it doing, do you think?" said the moth.

"Maybe it's lost?" said the first voice.

"Maybe it's sleepwalking?" said the second.

Margaret thought about this. But when she rubbed her eyes and gave her arm a good pinch, she seemed to be very much awake. She bent down to get a closer look at the moth, and the moth flattened its wings against the tree branch and held perfectly still.

For several moments, neither of them moved.

"Do you think …" the moth said at last, "do you think maybe it's *listening* to us?"

"Of course I am," Margaret said.

The moth gave a shout of surprise, fluttering into the air.

"Quick, Pip!" cried the second voice from up above. "It's probably planning to gobble you up!"

"No I'm not!" said Margaret.

"Get away from it, Pip!" said the first voice. "If we leave it alone, it'll have to go away."

But the moth called Pip had landed on the tree trunk just above Margaret's head and was looking down at her curiously.

"I don't know," said the moth. "It doesn't look so bad to me. Why don't we try talking to it?"

"We can't do that!"

"I'm not going to hurt you," said Margaret.

"You keep away from him!" cried the first voice. "See, Pip, you're encouraging it. Don't say another word!"

But as Margaret watched, the small moth fluttered lower down, settling in a sliver of moonlight near her face.

She could see now that he had two glittering, unblinking eyes, a pair of waving feelers that were reaching out toward her, three pairs of legs and two beautiful dusty gray wings. His head was cocked on one side, and he seemed to be studying Margaret's features just as she was studying his.

"I'm Margaret," said Margaret, remembering her manners.

"Pipperflit," said the moth, with a flit of his wings. "But you can call me Pip. You're not going to gobble me up, are you?"

"No, of course not!" said Margaret.

"Good," said Pip. "You know, I didn't think humans could hear us."

"I didn't think moths could talk," said Margaret.

"Didn't you? How funny!" The moth crawled along a branch until he was perched right in front of Margaret's nose. "Where did you come from?" he said.

"From the orphanage."

"Oh," said Pip. He was silent for a moment, and then nodded quickly. "Oh, yes, the orfallidge. I see. What's that?"

"It's a place for orphans. Children with no parents."

Pip looked up at her in amazement. "No parents!" he cried. "But where in the world did you come from?"

"No, no!" Margaret said. "We *had* parents once, just not anymore. Now we only have the Switch."

"Oh, yes, the Switch. I understand," said Pip, nodding. Then a few moments later, "What's a Switch?"

"She's horrible," Margaret said.

Just then, two more moths came fluttering down from the upper branches of the tree.

"Now you've done it!" one of them said, fluttering its wings in agitation. "Now that you've talked to it, it will probably stay here forever!"

"Don't be such a stinkbeetle!" said Pip. "I'm only being friendly. Anyway, it's called *Margaret*. This is Rimblewisp, and that's Flitterwing," said Pip to Margaret. "Rimb and Flit for short."

The two new moths landed on the branch, then tilted their heads to one side just as Pip had done.

"Whatsit?" said Flit.

"Hmph," said Rimb. "Why's it so big?"

"Hello," said Margaret, feeling rather silly. "I won't stay forever. I promise."

"There, you see!" said Pip. "It's only visiting."

"Well, it still seems very odd. Where did it come from?"

"The orfallidge," Pip said.

"Oh," said Rimb. The moth named Flit nodded.

Margaret only smiled. And as she sat there in the tree, talking with the moths in the dark of night, Margaret Grey became one of the few people in the world ever to discover the truth about moths.

CHAPTER 16

THE TRUTH ABOUT MOTHS

While the sight of a butterfly sets people to skipping around with nets, the sight of a moth most often inspires shrieks and fainting fits. Indeed, you may think that moths are nothing more than unfashionable butterflies — drab, ugly creatures to be ignored or run away from. But the truth about moths is much more wonderful.

If you were to sit and watch a moth for a whole day, it might look as if it were doing nothing at all. But the *night* is a different matter entirely. Nighttime is when the moths come alive.

As soon as the sun has set and the moths emerge from their nooks and corners, they have only one purpose until the next day's sunrise: to have as much fun as they possibly can.

They will play and fly and flutter in the moonlight until they are nearly breathless, stopping only for a sip of nectar or a drop of dew, then they will loop and spin and whirl until they're ready to collapse with happiness. So you can't blame them, really, for being quite tired out by morning, content to rest up quietly until the next night's festivities.

The other thing that moths are doing in the daytime is thinking up clever new games to impress their friends. Moths are very competitive, you see, and love nothing more than to show off.

You may have seen them at a game called Light-Hopping, which is one of the oldest and most popular moth games. Every time a moth spots a light or a lamppost, he will race to it as fast as possible. The last one to hop on the light is It, and that moth has to tag one of his friends, do three quick loop-de-loops and touch the light again before his friend can tag him back. This game is so popular that moths will even practice at it all alone, just to be ready when the time comes for a real match. And it is so popular that even the rumors of great danger posed by mysterious lights known as *candles* cannot stop them from playing it.

They have other games, too. There is Hoverpik, where moths fly in formation to make shapes that the others guess at, and Billabump, which is a flying form of leapfrog. In fact, Margaret had interrupted a game of Billabump between Pip, Rimb and Flit that was taking place on the lawn. When the three moths had heard Margaret's footsteps approaching, they'd abandoned their game and fled into the tree.

There are very few events that can cause moths to abandon a game before it's finished. On rare occasions, a silently swooping owl or a sudden hailstorm might cause moths to take cover inside their tree.

On one infamous night many years before, a barefoot dreg named Sally Winkleson had shuffled through the yard in her nightgown, fast asleep. She had walked straight through a game of Hoverpik, stopped in her tracks, and then turned around and marched back to the orphanage, pausing once to ask, "Which way to the cheese factory?" But the appearance of Margaret, wide-awake and curious, was the first of its kind.

These were some of the marvelous things she discovered listening to Pip, Rimb and Flit, as she took in the sights and sounds of the moth tree for the first time.

"Games afoot!" called a voice suddenly from outside. "Whirlawhoomps!"

The wings of the three moths began to twitch. Then, without a word, they flew upward out of the branches and into the night.

Margaret scrambled after them, back through the makeshift tunnel in the brush. And what she saw when she emerged made her gasp for the second time that night.

More moths had come out of hiding. There were dozens, maybe hundreds of them, flitting through the air in chaotic loops and twirls. The sky was alive with moths at play.

At first she didn't see a pattern in it, but after sitting

quietly for a few minutes, she began to understand.

Whirlawhoomps is a moth game played late in the spring, when the most impatient of the moths have emerged from their cocoons and the slow movers are still enjoying their time as caterpillars.

To play, each moth pairs up with a caterpillar, who spins a small thread of silk. Together they fasten one end of the thread around a small blue berry, which the moths call Plurpils. Once the Plurpil is fastened, the moth carries the other end of the thread with its front legs and takes off into the air.

And that is when the fun really starts.

The goal of Whirlawhoomps is to swing your Plurpil so that it squishes into another moth, marking them with blue juice. As soon as that happens, the moth who has been squished on is Out for the rest of the round, and the moth who's done the squishing zips off to look for their next target.

Margaret, sitting cross-legged at the foot of the brush, hardly knew where to look. Her eyes darted between loop-de-loops, and swinging Plurpils, and zooming and zipping moths. She popped a handful of Plurpils into her mouth from time to time, and they tasted tangy and sweet. She sat there quietly in the grass for what seemed like no time at all, until finally she began to yawn. Only then did she notice the dawn creeping over the horizon.

"Oh!" she said, jumping to her feet. "I should go."

"Why?" said Pip. "The game's not over."

"I'm sorry, but I need to get back."

"Back to the orfallidge?" piped up Flit.

"Yes," said Margaret. "Back there."

"See you, Whatsit!" said Flit.

"You'll come back tomorrow, won't you, Margaret?" said Pip.

Margaret smiled. "I will," she said.

And she ran back to the orphanage.

CHAPTER 17

SANCTUARY

The Margaret Grey who climbed back into bed was not the same Margaret Grey who had snuck away from the orphanage in the dead of night a few short hours before. Even though her eyes were still tired, her clothes were still gray and scratchy and her stomach was still hungry, Margaret had changed on the inside.

Now she had a secret, which was something Switch couldn't take away from her. From that day onward, Margaret crept from her bed every night and ran softly out of the orphanage to meet with Pip and the other moths. And in those few wonderful hours before she collapsed back to sleep, she could forget about her life of drudgery.

"It's Margaret of the orfallidge!" Pip would cry when he saw her coming, and he and the other moths would welcome her into the tree as if she were a very large and distant cousin.

Margaret's secret made her daytime hours more bearable, too.

Even as she was forced to use a moldy toothbrush to scrape gunk out from between the kitchen tiles, she imagined she was crawling through the thorny tunnel to the moth tree. Even as she forced spoonfuls of cold mush into her mouth, she remembered the taste of the tangy blue Plurpils. And even as she spent hours beating dust out of the curtains with a large racket, she imagined she was talking with Pip, and everything seemed much better.

Any place you can go to escape from the pinches and punishments of the world is called a sanctuary, and this is just what Margaret had found in the moth tree. But the trouble with sanctuaries is that sooner or later you have to leave them.

One blustery morning when Margaret was put on mush-making duty in the kitchen, something happened that pulled her out of hers.

Mush making was a particularly boring chore that involved taking big bricks of packed oats, squishing them in a bowl, and pouring warm water onto them to make the tasteless mush that was served to the dregs at mealtimes.

Margaret was sitting on a small stool, squishing oats and thinking of the previous night's game of Hoverpik, when an enormous crash shattered the silence in the kitchen. Looking over, she saw a terrified red-haired girl holding a silver tray and standing over a mess of broken china.

"You clumsy lunkhead!" shouted Lacey, who appeared a moment later from the hall. "You've done it now! Miss Switch will have your skin for this!" Grabbing the girl by one ear, she dragged her out of the room.

Margaret and the other children followed, keeping a safe distance. When they reached the front hall, Lacey began shrieking at the top of her lungs up the stairs. "Miss Switch! Miss Switch, come quickly!"

After a few moments, a door opened somewhere on the upper floor and Miss Switch swept into view at the top of the staircase. "Lacey, dear," she said, her eyes gleaming. "What have I told you about shouting?"

"This dreg ruined your china tea set, Miss Switch!" Lacey said quickly, shoving the red-haired girl forward. "The stupid scab smashed it!"

Switch shot an icy glare at the unfortunate girl. "Sarah Pottley, isn't it?" Her voice grew horribly quiet. "This isn't the first time we've suffered from your buffoonery." A dead silence fell across the room, and all eyes turned toward Switch.

"I'm — I'm sorry," Sarah was spluttering, her eyes wide with terror. "So s-s-sorry!"

Miss Switch raised one perfectly manicured finger, and the girl fell silent. "I think, my dear," she said, gliding slowly down the stairs, "that you need to be taught a lesson."

"Please!" begged Sarah Pottley, her whole body trembling. "Please, no!"

Miss Switch smiled a terrible smile. "But my dear child," she said, her voice mocking and sickly sweet. "How else will anything get through that thick head of yours?" Darting down the remaining stairs, she grasped the trembling girl by the arm. "Come along, children. We're going *up*."

With a few strides of her long legs, Switch pulled the unfortunate Sarah Pottley up the stairs and around the corner. The other children ran to keep up as she strode down the hall, past the orphans' bedrooms and up another flight of stairs.

"Where's she going?" Margaret heard someone whisper behind her.

"The attic," she heard Judy answer.

"Oh, no!" another boy gasped. "Not the window!"

Spanning the attic wall was an enormous window, which Switch threw open to reveal the steep drop down to the yard below. A strong cold wind came whipping in. Still smiling her malicious smile, the Matron pushed Sarah Pottley toward the open window.

"Now," Switch hissed with delight. "Out you go, dreg."

Shaking uncontrollably, Sarah took a step forward and then turned back in fear. "Please," she begged. "D-don't make me —"

"You have to learn, my dear, the dangers of smashing things to smithereens on the ground," Switch said. When the girl still didn't move, Switch raised her voice to a terrible pitch and shouted, "*Out!*"

Bursting into tears, Sarah took one shaky step, then another, then reached out a hand to grab hold of the windowsill and hoist herself onto the ledge.

"Almost there," Switch said. Then with a sudden thrust, she pushed Sarah over the ledge. The children gasped, and Sarah screamed as she plummeted out of the window.

"No!" Margaret barely stopped herself from crying aloud. But when she rushed forward with the rest of the children to peer over the sill, she saw that Sarah had landed on a small ledge that jutted out from the building.

"Pull me back!" Sarah cried, her frizzy red hair whipping in the strong wind. "Please, I'm going to slip!"

"You should be fine if you hold very still," Switch said gleefully, "and keep your stupid mouth shut."

"The wind is too strong!" Sarah shouted, and Margaret could see that powerful gusts were pushing and pulling at the frantic girl, making her sway alarmingly.

"Don't be so dramatic," Switch said, her smile widening. "I think this is the perfect place for you to stand quietly and think about what you've done."

Margaret looked around the attic and saw that the other orphans were watching Sarah's plight in helpless silence.

"Please!" Sarah Pottley's voice cried again. "Somebody help!"

But for poor Sarah Pottley, there was no help to be found. There was only the Switch. Turning back to the horrified children, the Matron beckoned Lacey to her side. "You can let her in," the Switch said, her voice cool, "after sundown."

"Yes, Miss Switch." Lacey gave a small curtsy as Miss Switch swept back down the stairs. Then with a satisfied glare at the rest of the children, Lacey pulled the window shutters closed with a bang.

"Back to work, dregs!" she snarled, shoving them down the attic stairs.

Back to work they went, quiet and fearful. And for the rest of the day, they tried in vain to ignore the cries of distress that drifted down from the attic.

Even Margaret, with her secret supply of happy thoughts, couldn't block out the distant screams. Sarah Pottley's torment had intruded on her sanctuary.

Margaret's heart filled with sadness at each pitiful wail, because while Margaret was lucky enough to have a wonderful secret all her own, she knew Sarah Pottley had nothing to distract herself from the thought of being smashed to smithereens.

This quality is one of the basic ways to spot good people with kind hearts. It is called sympathy, and people who have it make up for all the bullies of this world, who feel nothing at all.

CHAPTER 18

A RUN OF BAD LUCK

When Margaret ran to the moth tree that night, she could barely contain the awful feelings that had stayed with her all through the day. Bursting through the tunnel in the brush, she told Pip exactly what Switch had done to poor Sarah Pottley.

"That stinkbeetle! That swindleswine!" he cried, zipping around in a fury.

Margaret nodded grimly. Switch had spent the afternoon catching up on her reading, reclining on a silk chaise with a large stack of fashion magazines. To all appearances, she was completely unmoved by the cries of fear that drifted down from above, her only reaction to each of the unfortunate dreg's wails being a casual flip of a glossy page.

As Margaret described the whole of that dreadful day, Pip grew very quiet, his wings twitching as though he were about to fly off for a game of Billabump.

"Dungwaddler!" he cried instead. "That's what she is!"

He flitted around the tree, hurling more and more insults at the absent Switch, until Margaret grinned in spite of herself.

· Calling the Matron names was something Margaret had never thought she would do, as Great-aunt Linda had taught her never to criticize her elders. But when dealing with an elder who is also a terrifying bully, a good bout of name calling can be a very useful exercise. This is because as soon as you can laugh at a thing you've been afraid of, you begin to whittle away at its fearsomeness.

The more insults Pip hurled at Switch, 'the less gloomy Margaret's mood became. Her grin grew into a wide smile, and her smile burst into a giggle. And soon, in the very spot in her mind where her fear of Switch had been, Margaret found there was no fear at all. In its place was something she hadn't felt in a very long time: a glimmering bit of hope.

Sometimes, improving things just a little makes a great deal of difference. It occurred to Margaret that if the other orphans could only laugh, perhaps they, too, could be a little less afraid. Perhaps the gloom of the Hopeton Orphanage could be broken, even if just for a moment. And as Margaret imagined grins and smiles on the faces of the other orphans, she knew just what would make them smile the most.

There was one person who deserved to be laughed at more than any other: the same person who had laughed at each of *them* so often. The same person who had tricked and taunted and tortured them, and kept every good thing for herself.

Margaret decided it was time for things to change. And she thought she knew exactly how to manage it.

"Magazines," she said aloud.

"What's that?" said Pip.

A great and clever plan had formed in Margaret's head.

~~~

Each morning after breakfast, Miss Switch would go into her study and read a stack of fashion magazines. And every time she opened a shiny new magazine, she always flipped right to the back to check the horoscopes.

A horoscope, in case you didn't know, is an extremely vague piece of advice given from one perfect stranger to another. While any reasonable person knows to pay horoscopes no attention at all, gullible people will always obey them no matter how silly their advice may be.

It was well known among the orphans that Switch took her horoscopes very seriously, and it was this fact that formed the basis of Margaret's great and clever plan.

Before the night was through, she had crept to Switch's study and scooped up a large stack of old magazines. She sacrificed her few hours of sleep to search through the horoscopes with Pip, and by sunrise they had found exactly the ones they needed. Tearing out the pages very carefully, Margaret tucked them into the sleeve of her dress.

When the mailman arrived that morning, leaving Switch's new magazines on the front doorstep, Margaret was there to snatch them up. She clipped out the horoscope pages, and with the glue that Switch sometimes used to stick children's hands together, she pasted the old ones in their place.

The first horoscope now read, "Bad luck awaits if the little things distract you."

The second one said, "See a penny, pick it up."

And the last horoscope said, "Climb to the highest peak."

These were the messages Miss Switch read in her study that day, after Margaret had replaced the glossy magazines on the doorstep.

And Miss Switch, who was always on the lookout for bad luck, read them over three times.

It just so happened that her peaceful reading was interrupted very suddenly by a loud clattering noise outside her study door. When Switch threw the door open, she saw tiny Timothy Smealing struggling with a large tray of noisy dishes.

"The little things ..." she hissed, remembering her horoscope and realizing with horror that she'd just been distracted by one.

"Lacey!" she shrieked. "Dregs! Listen up. If I hear so much as a peep or see so much as a finger from any of you today, I'll tie your feet to the ceiling like mistletoe and leave you there for a week! I don't want to be distracted by a single one of you! Is that understood?"

"Yes, Miss Switch," chimed the children.

"Was that a peep?!" screeched the Switch. "I can still see you!"

Without another word, the children bolted from sight.

Miss Switch sighed. "Much better," she said to no one. "Don't any of you show your spotty faces again until tomorrow morning. *Or else.*"

None of the orphans made even the smallest sound in response.

The rest of the day consisted of a great deal of hiding and shushing among the orphans as Miss Switch moved through different rooms of the house.

Nothing interesting happened until just after dinnertime, when Miss Switch went upstairs for a soak in her private bathtub. The children who had been hiding in the kitchen slowly came out from behind their curtains and cupboards and began quietly preparing their dinners of cold mush.

But Margaret was doing something else. She was waiting just outside Switch's bedroom door, holding a small handful of pennies she'd collected from a crow's nest in the brush.

When she heard the Matron's footsteps approaching, she placed a single shiny penny just outside Switch's door and sprinted down the hall in the direction of the attic.

When Switch reached the top of the stairs, her

eyes fell on the penny. She snatched it up greedily, remembering her horoscope, and just as she did so she noticed another penny lying only a few feet away.

"How delightful!" she said aloud, feeling sure that if one penny was good luck, two would be even better. She picked up the second penny, only to spot another tiny glint farther down the hall by the attic stairs. She was just pocketing the third penny, when another caught the light a few stairs up.

Switch followed the trail of pennies, feeling both incredibly lucky and vaguely surprised that she had never noticed so many pennies lying around before. Then she came to a penny in the middle of the attic floor. It seemed to be the last one, and it was sitting next to the ladder that led up to the roof.

Margaret, who was watching from behind a dusty old wardrobe, held her breath to see if the last part of her plan would work.

Switch looked to the right, then the left, then directly behind her. And then she remembered what her last horoscope had said.

Climb to the highest peak.

She looked up.

The trapdoor to the roof was directly above her head. It had a long string attached to the handle so that you could pull the door closed from inside, and the string was swaying slowly back and forth in a draft of cold air.

Without a moment's thought, Miss Switch climbed up the ladder and pushed open the trapdoor.

Leaving Margaret's shoulder, Pip flew after the Matron as she stepped onto the windy roof and began scanning for pennies. The moment her back was turned to the trapdoor, he zipped back inside.

"Now!" he cried.

Miss Switch, of course, couldn't hear him. But Margaret could.

She dashed across the attic to the ladder, climbed up it, and yanked hard on the dangling string. The trapdoor came slamming down with a bang, and Margaret slid the latch that locked it from the inside.

The Switch was trapped! And as Margaret darted back to her hiding place, she could hear the Matron screaming to be let back in.

When the other orphans began tiptoeing up to the attic to see what all the ruckus was about, Margaret stepped out from behind the wardrobe and blended into the back of the growing crowd.

"You, dreg!" Lacey hissed, pointing at Judy. "Go up there and see what Miss Switch wants."

"She said she didn't want to see us," Judy said, shaking her head. "She said she'd hang us up like mistletoe."

And though Lacey kept trying to get the dregs to open the door, she didn't dare do it herself for fear of disobeying Miss Switch's orders.

It is a very satisfying thing to see people get a taste of their own medicine. Even though Switch screamed like a banshee all through the rainy night, and even though her fancy gown was soaked through, and even though the next morning she was hacking and sneezing with a terrible cold, there was no one for her to punish. They had all, as Lacey explained nervously when she let Switch in, only been following the Matron's own command.

By mid-morning chores, the tale had become very popular.

"The whole night!" whispered Vickram Skitter.

"In the rain," whispered Phoebe Frizzleton.

"In her evening dress!" giggled Bessie Blotchly.

The rooftop story was told again and again, and every time, it brought little smiles to the faces of the orphans.

And early the next morning when the mailman came by, he wondered why the trash cans were so full of magazines.

CHAPTER 19

THE NIMBLERS

When Margaret Grey was growing up, she had all the exciting "firsts" that other children have.

There was the first time she read a book by herself, the first time she tied her own shoes and the first time she wrote the alphabet in cursive letters. But every time Margaret did one of these clever things and toddled over to inform her aunt, Great-aunt Linda would tell her not to blow her own horn. This had confused Margaret at first, since she couldn't play the horn or any other musical instrument.

What Great-aunt Linda had meant is that small children shouldn't brag about their accomplishments. Bragging and boasting and blowing your own horn all mean the same thing, but no matter what you call it, it was a thing young Margaret was never allowed to do.

When the rooftop plot went off without a hitch, Margaret felt enormously happy and relieved. But even if she hadn't been forbidden to speak to the other orphans, it would never have occurred to her to blow her own horn.

"It's Whatsit!" shrieked Flit, when Margaret crawled through the tunnel to the moth tree the following night.

"Margaret?" came Pip's voice from up in the tree.

"Hello!" Margaret called, climbing up to him.

As she settled herself on a sturdy branch, letting her legs dangle, she saw that Pip was surrounded by a group of moths. They all seemed to be waiting for her, and they all looked very excited.

"Margaret's here!"

"Let's hear the story!"

"She's *my* Margaret," Pip said importantly, taking his place on her shoulder, "so I'll be the one to ask. Tell the story, Margaret!"

Contrary to Great-aunt Linda's idea of correct manners, in the moth world, blowing your own horn is not at all impolite. In fact, it is expected. After a round of Billabump or Light-Hopping or Whirlawhoomps, moths will sit around and brag about their brilliance for hours on end. A good boaster is highly respected, because in the moth world boasting is really like a game in itself.

Encouraged by Pip, Margaret launched into the tale of Switch on the roof. As she told her story, the crowd of moths grew so that soon the entire tree had gathered to hear her.

"Nicely played!" said a moth called Milliwisp, when she came to the end.

"Well snuck!" said a moth called Putterwing.

"I was there, too!" said Pip. He was just explaining the important role he had played with the trapdoor, when he stopped speaking very suddenly. He was perfectly still for several seconds. And then his wings began to twitch.

"What's wrong?" said Margaret.

Looking around, she noticed that all the other moths had frozen, too, their wings quivering with energy just like Pip's. Then, everyone began talking at once.

"They're back!"

"Good Nimblers tonight!"

"What's going on?" said Margaret.

"Can't you smell them?" said Pip.

Margaret sniffed the air, but all she could smell was the pleasant mossy scent of the green dome. She frowned and looked back at Pip, but he was gone.

In seconds, the tree had come alive with moths flying up from every branch. They zipped away through the branches to the outside, until only Margaret and the caterpillars were left.

Margaret jumped down from her branch and scrambled through the tunnel. When she emerged onto the grass, the moths were shouting and laughing together in a great busy cloud.

"I smell a good one!"

"Quick, catch it!"

"Mmm! Tasty!"

High in the air, the moths looped and zigzagged in unison, as if they were chasing some invisible thing.

Margaret gazed up at the beautiful sight, watching in wonder for several minutes.

She was still trying to make out what the game was, when the strange chase ended as suddenly as it had begun. The pattern broke apart and, one by one, the moths turned to head back to the tree.

"What was that all about?" asked Margaret, as Pip fluttered down to sit on her shoulder.

"Didn't you see the Nimblers?" said Pip, as if she ought to know what that meant. "They were delicious tonight!"

Margaret shrugged. "What's a Nimbler?"

"Don't you know?"

She shook her head.

"How funny! A Nimbler is — well it's a sort of shimmery cloud thing. You have to be nimbler than it is if you want to catch it."

"You eat them?" said Margaret.

"What else would we do with them?" said Pip. "They're scrumptious! Much better than nectar."

"What do they taste like?"

"Oh, all sorts of things. Honey and pinecones and berries, and cinnamon and licorice and peppermint ..."

Uncoiling his straw-like tongue, Pip made a hungry, slurping noise. Margaret felt her own mouth watering.

"We hadn't had good ones in ages, only rotten ones. Those kind make you sick. Then last night when I got back from your orfallidge, the sky was full of tasty ones! And again tonight!"

"I still don't understand," she said. "What *are* they?"

"Well, they come from your head, don't they?"

"They what?!" cried Margaret.

"You know," Pip said. "Humans and dogs and bears and creatures like that. They come from your head when you're deep asleep. When you're tossing and turning and muttering to yourself."

"Oh," said Margaret slowly. "Do you mean a dream?"

"I don't know," said Pip. "Do they float up and dance around in the air?"

"I didn't think they did," said Margaret, feeling rather amazed.

But of course, it's nearly impossible to watch yourself sleeping, as anyone who's tried will know. Even if you could watch yourself sleep, you still wouldn't be able to see what the moths see.

Margaret had discovered at last the most important truth about moths. They are good at games and good at doing nothing at all. They are good at being happy and good at laughing. They are skilled boasters, and they are wonderfully good listeners.

But of all the wonderful truths about them, the most wonderful is this: they are the only creatures to know the colors and tastes of dreams.

CHAPTER 20

THE PETTISH DREG

Miss Switch had ordered that no one was permitted to speak of her night on the rooftop ever again. And yet, to her deep annoyance, she had a strange suspicion that her orders were being disobeyed.

She couldn't help noticing that there was altogether too much giggling and smiling going on. Too much disgusting cheeriness. It simply wouldn't do.

Try as she might to forget her humiliation, every giggle and grin was a tiny reminder of the rain-soaked rooftop, and these reminders put her in a very foul mood indeed.

As you know, Switch liked to divide the world neatly into two groups: those with her own divine good looks and those without. You also know that she always judged people on first impressions. What you have yet to know, however, is that just as the existence of the dreggish Pet Agatha Spink always nagged at the back of Switch's mind, there was also a Pettish dreg in the orphanage whose presence unnerved her even more.

Helen Ravish was a sweet-tempered girl with very long, very lovely hair. But on the day she arrived at the Hopeton Orphanage, her mouth had sprouted cold sores, her long hair was a matted nest and her eyes were bright red from crying over the loss of her parents. So it was only fitting that Switch had her thrown in with the rest of the dregs.

But the problem was, Helen Ravish was rather nice looking now. Even nicer looking than many of the Pets. This complicated things terribly for Switch, who couldn't help but admire Helen's lovely hair but was never able to admit it.

Helen had no way of knowing just how much her lovely hair irked the Matron. And she had no way of knowing that wearing her hair in a beautiful plaited braid was the worst thing she could have possibly done after Switch's ordeal on the roof. But just because you have no way of knowing something doesn't mean you won't get walloped for it.

Two days after the embarrassment of the rooftop, Helen was sent upstairs with a basket of ribbons and bows, which she carried to Switch's private sitting room. Lacey and two other Pets were on sewing duty, pinning the seam of a dress. And Miss Switch, who was in the dress, happened to look down just as Helen entered the room.

"Scat, dreg," mumbled Lacey, who had a needle between her teeth.

Helen set down the basket and turned to leave.

"What a lovely braid, Helen," purred Miss Switch.

"Thank you," said Helen very quietly.

"It looks quite pretty, don't you think?"

"Yes," said Helen, and then she clapped her hand over her mouth, realizing what she'd just said.

"So," said the Switch. "You think you look pretty, then? You think that a dreg like you is allowed to be pretty?"

"No — no, I don't!" said Helen, beginning to tremble.

Switch took a step forward, knocking the Pets and their sewing needles to the ground. She looked into Helen's frightened eyes, and Helen saw the Matron's face darken like an angry thundercloud.

"You probably think you're quite fashionable," said the Switch very quietly. Reaching a hand into the sewing basket, she removed a pair of long silver scissors.

Then in one swift movement, she grabbed Helen's braid. And with sudden, violent snips, she chopped off all of Helen's lovely hair, right to the scalp.

"That's much better," she said, nudging Helen toward the mirror. "Much more suitable for a dreg."

Helen cried out as she caught a look at her reflection. All that was left of her lovely hair were a few spiky tufts that stuck out in all directions.

Lacey, whose hair was rather stringy, and who had always secretly envied the dreg, shrieked with delight.

Miss Switch smiled the smile of a bully happy to be back in practice.

"Dregs really don't know much about fashion, do they?" she said in her sweetest purr, handing Helen the limp braid.

"No, Miss Switch," whispered Helen through her tears.

The debraiding of Helen Ravish had just the effect on the other orphans that Switch wanted. The giggles hushed, the smiles faded away and the atmosphere of fear returned. Things were just as dreadful as they had been before.

But Margaret wasn't fearful. Just as soon as she could, she raced out to the moth tree to tell Pip what had happened.

"That wallyscag!" Pip cried angrily as Margaret finished her tale.

Margaret nodded in agreement.

Some people, when faced with a series of defeats, might choose to turn tail and put thoughts of victory behind them. But whether it was Pip's indignation or an anger all her own, Margaret was determined not to let Switch get away with the things she had done.

If your parents have any taste in bedtime stories, you may have heard of a green-capped bandit called Robin Hood, and how he stole things from rich people to give them away to the poor. On the surface, Robin Hood was just a very famous robber. But since those he stole from were thieves themselves, most people thought he deserved a pat on the back rather than a prison sentence.

Like stealing from thieves, whether it is right or wrong to seek revenge against a bully really depends on how you look at it. And as Margaret crept down the basement stairs that night, with Pip on her shoulder and a new plan brewing in her mind, she looked at her task as a very noble one indeed.

With Pip flying ahead to check that the coast was clear, she made her way down the stairs to a storage room deep under the orphanage.

"Just a little should do it," said Margaret to Pip, as they peered into the large sack of powder that was used to mix dyes for the orphans' clothes.

Then, reaching her hand into the sack, she drew out a handful of fine gray powder.

CHAPTER 21

A TOUCH OF GRAY

Apart from thinking up creative new ways to terrorize dregs, Switch spent her days in a very particular way.

The thing she was most particular about was making her *toilette*, which is a French word for spending a ridiculous amount of time in front of a mirror trying to make yourself look attractive.

Switch made her *toilette* in an enormous bathroom with mirrors from floor to ceiling, which was full of hundreds of combs, brushes, bottles, vials, tubes, jars and pots. All morning long, a procession of Pets went in and out, working to prink and preen and prettify her. Her creamy skin was rinsed and powdered, her golden hair was lathered and brushed, her makeup alone took over two hours. Every single inch of her, from the top of her head to the tips of her toenails, had its own special treatment. What she looked like without the many layers of powder and makeup, no one knew.

On delivery days, the mailman would bring boxes of fresh beauty supplies to the orphanage, and Lacey and another Pet called Emily Darlington would unpack them in Switch's bathroom.

The boxes were labelled "For the Foundlings," which made the mailman think they contained clothes and books and toys for the poor dear orphans.

"What a very kind woman," he always said to himself as he continued on his rounds. Little did he know that the very kind woman was having her toenails filed by a poor dear orphan while sipping on a cocktail and reading about the latest trends in handbags.

As it happened, the day after the debraiding of Helen Ravish was a delivery day.

"Look what you've done, dolt!" Lacey yelled, as she unpacked the boxes that morning.

"Sorry! Oopsie!" chirped Emily Darlington.

Emily, with her bouncy blonde ringlets and rosy cheeks, was perhaps the most adorable child in the whole orphanage, but she was also one of the dimmest.

She had been midway through refilling Switch's shampoo bottle when she had stopped to stare at a crystal vial of perfume on the countertop. The light from the bathroom window shone onto the crystal, casting little rainbows around the room.

"Oh, pretty!" Emily had murmured, letting the shampoo run into her lap and onto the bathroom floor.

"You're the most doltish dolt in this whole stinking place!" Lacey shouted.

"I'm sorry, Lacey."

"Clean up this mess! And you can finish these boxes by yourself."

Lacey called Emily a dolt a few more times for good measure, then stomped out of the room to find a dreg to pick on. This was Lacey's favorite way to do chores, as she preferred to take credit for other people's work if it was done well, and punish them if it was not.

Emily sat and looked around at all the work she had to do, biting her tongue between her teeth like a kitten. A few moments later, Margaret appeared.

Neither Lacey nor the doltish Emily had noticed Pip keeping watch from the windowsill, waiting for a moment just like this one. And Margaret, her talented ears listening for his call, had hurried to the bathroom just as Lacey left.

"Hello!" said Margaret, stepping in between two tall mirrors so that her reflection multiplied all around the mirrored room.

"Hello!" said Emily, jumping to her feet. "Wait ..." She wrinkled her brow in confusion. "I'm not supposed to talk to dregs."

"You're not talking to a dreg," said Margaret.

"I'm not?" said Emily, arching a pretty pointed eyebrow.

"No, the dregs aren't allowed in here. I'm your reflection."

"Oh ..." Emily looked around at all the Margarets. She raised her right arm above her head very slowly, and Margaret did the exact same thing with her left.

"Fun!" laughed Emily, continuing the game with her other hand.

Margaret mirrored the Pet's movements for a minute or so, collapsing to the ground convincingly when Emily tried to lift both her little feet in the air at the same time.

"Not the brightest, is she?" said Pip, and Margaret tried not to smile.

"What are all those?" Margaret asked when she and Emily had righted themselves, pointing to the jars and bottles all over the floor.

"These are Miss Switch's."

"Yes, but what are they for?"

"Well, this one's hand cream, this one's face powder, this one's hair tonic and —"

But the Pet broke off.

At a small nod from Margaret, tinkling music had started to play from a beautiful ballerina music box on the counter.

"Oh, pretty!" said Emily. She skipped toward it, her blonde curls bobbing.

If you had been in Switch's bathroom, you would have seen Pip flying away from the music box lever and a quick movement of Margaret's hand over the bottle of hair tonic at the very moment Emily turned away. But Emily, bless her, saw nothing but the graceful twirls of the clockwork ballet dancer.

When the dancer stopped spinning a few minutes later and Emily Darlington returned to her boxes and bottles, the mysterious reflection was gone. Unconcerned, Emily went about her work and soon forgot about the whole encounter, save for the song of the music-box ballerina, which she continued to hum for the rest of the day.

The next morning, however, the residents of the Hopeton Orphanage were woken by an ear-splitting, spine-chilling, blood-curdling cry of rage.

"GRAAAAAARRRGGG!"

The dregs heard it and sat bolt upright in their beds. The Pets heard it and sat bolt upright in theirs. The mouth of every orphan fell open and stayed frozen that way, because Switch was yelling as they had never heard her yell before. Even Margaret, with her finely tuned listening, could only make out the odd word, like "treachery!" "bottle!" and "vengeance!"

After one long, drawn-out scream from Switch, the orphans heard the shattering sound of mirrors being smashed. Then, with angry stomps that came closer and closer, Switch came shrieking down the hall.

As she passed the dregs' doorway, they saw that she was wearing a giant silk scarf wrapped around her head like a massive beehive. Her shrieking continued down the stairs, and a few moments later came the slamming of the front door and the screeching of tires.

The dregs sprang from their beds to the windows just in time to see a small convertible speed away from the house. And as the car took off down the dusty road, Switch's silk scarf came loose and flew off.

Of course, you have probably already guessed what it was hiding. Streaming from Switch's head, whipping through the air, was a headful of frizzled gray hair.

"Oh!" gasped Judy.

"Hee hee!" chuckled Phoebe.

"HA!" snickered Vickram.

Sarah Pottley rubbed her eyes.

Margaret just smiled, watching the scarf flutter down to land in the dust.

It is not, generally speaking, very nice to be pleased about someone else's misfortunes. But when that someone is a horrible and vain bully, it can be very hard to stop yourself.

PART THREE

THE DREAMS

CHAPTER 22

FURY FOILED

Nine times out of ten, the saying "Better late than never" makes very little sense. Most of the time, doing something too late is just as bad as never doing it at all.

There is very little point, for example, in stepping on the brakes after you've driven your car off the edge of a cliff. It is also rather pointless to show up for your wedding two years after the date written on the invitations. And if you were delivering a pardon from the king for someone on their way to the gallows, arriving late would be just as bad as never coming at all.

Some people, though, put a lot of stock in this phrase.

Great-aunt Linda, for instance, had used it every Tuesday when her backgammon tournament ran late and Margaret had to wait an extra three hours for supper.

And Miss Switch, who preferred to punish dregs in a timely manner whenever possible, was saying it over and over to herself as she sat in a beauty parlor with her head slathered in thick purple goop.

When she finally reappeared in the doorway of the orphanage seven hours later, her hair had been restored to a beautiful, silky blonde, and her face was as composed and flawless as ever. But her glittering eyes were seething with fury. And her mind was made up that when it came to punishments, they were most definitely better late than never.

As Switch began her interrogations, however, it soon became clear that her fury had nowhere to go.

Lacey explained that she had taken the boxes straight from the mailman and left the task of unpacking them with doltish Emily Darlington.

Little Emily, on persistent questioning, said it must have been the mirror who tampered with the bottles, or perhaps the music-box ballerina.

"Oh — yes! The ballerina!" gasped Emily. And she began to hum softly to herself and twirl around.

Switch rolled her eyes, then turned her attention to the rest of the orphans, who were cowering around the room in terror.

"So," she said softly. "That's it, is it? No one can tell me how this little mistake may have taken place?"

No one spoke. Margaret, as you know, could easily have answered Switch's question. But as she was conveniently forbidden to make any noise, she kept her mouth tightly shut.

"Maybe ... the bottle?" Lacey said. "The mailman could've mixed up the delivery."

Switch stared at Lacey carefully for several moments. Then she glared at the others, whipped around, and began ascending the stairs. She was halfway up before she turned back to face them.

"There will be no supper tonight," she said, "and unless I change my mind, no food in the morning, either."

Lacey had just flashed her wide, hyena-like smile at the dregs when the Switch continued.

"No supper for *any* of you."

And turning again, she disappeared up the stairs.

Lacey's hyena grin melted off her face in disbelief.

In the whole history of the Hopeton Orphanage, only three Pets had ever been punished by Miss Switch.

The first was a sweet little lad called Milton Pinkrich, who had scribbled all over Switch's magazines thinking they were coloring books. When she saw what he had done, Switch scrawled "PEST" across his face in a rage, and it didn't wash off for a month.

The second was a delightfully handsome boy called Henry Fitzflatterly, who made the mistake of saying that Switch must have been the most beautiful girl in the world "in her youth." Switch taped his hands over his eyes and left them that way for three days, causing him to stumble around bumping into things.

And on the third occasion, a precious little girl called Agnes Primrose had the misfortune of calling the Matron "Mother" by accident. Switch made her walk around with a bar of soap in her mouth for a week.

But this latest punishment was entirely unprecedented.

Along with fashion, horoscopes and egg whites, you see, Switch was a great believer in cause and effect. Every bit of punishing the Switch had ever ordered had been, in her mind, exactly fitting to the crime of the offending orphan. But starving the lot of them for something they hadn't done wasn't fitting in the slightest. It was, for all but one of them, an effect without a cause.

So as the orphans stared up after their furious Matron, Pet and dreg alike wondered nervously what was going on in her head. Because each of them knew that a rule-breaking Switch was a very dangerous Switch indeed.

CHAPTER 23

TROUBLES GREAT AND TROUBLES SMALL

When the orphans climbed into their beds that night, not a single one of them fell asleep easily. The Pets tossed and turned with grumpiness, angry that their stomachs were growling just as much as the dregs'. The dregs tossed and turned in worry, anxious about the prospect of so many grumpy Pets. And everyone tossed and turned thinking about the furious and unpredictable Switch.

Because she had to wait for all the tossing and turning to quiet down, Margaret was later than usual slipping away to the yard.

And as she approached the grassy lawn, she found that things were uneasy there, too.

Instead of the shouts and cheers of tiny playful voices, the sounds that drifted toward her were sounds of alarm, and the scene that met her eyes as she drew nearer was one she had never seen before.

"Oh no!"

"Not again …"

"Moth down!"

A cluster of moths was flying across the lawn, carrying a leaf suspended by long silken threads. On the leaf was another, twitching moth. It was Flitterwing.

"Flit!" cried Margaret. "What's happened?"

She followed the moths through the tunnel and into the tree, where Flit's leaf was laid carefully down on an exposed root. A few fuzzy caterpillars came creeping down the tree bark, and from all over the tree, moths were hurrying from their nooks. They all began talking at once.

"He's had a bad one," one of them said.

"I was winning, you know!"

"Oh, be quiet!" said Rimblewisp, coming to land at Flit's side. "And don't crowd him." He paced along the leaf, looking down at his friend.

"Rimb, what happened?" said Margaret. "Is he very badly hurt?"

"Hmph!" grumbled Rimb. "It's his own fault. Silly twitterbug gobbled a bad one before smelling it properly."

"But *what's* he gobbled?" cried Margaret.

"A Nimbler," said Pip with a sigh, crawling onto Margaret's knee. "The good ones have dried up again! They've all gone sour."

The feelers of every moth drooped sadly as the moths fell to whispering, and Margaret leaned against the great wrinkled trunk, her mind whirring.

Chances are, you've already guessed what Margaret was thinking, because you are thinking it, too.

After Switch had been made ridiculous on the roof, and the children had slept happily in their beds after so many unhappy nights, the Nimblers had been suddenly sweet and good. But now, with the Switch more terrifying than ever, the dreams of the orphans had turned all to nightmares.

When the tree began to hum with talk again, Margaret looked up to see that Flit had stopped twitching and was sleeping peacefully.

The mood of the tree had shifted as though a storm cloud had passed overhead, and the moths were soon laughing and fluttering as though nothing had happened. They must, Margaret realized, have done this many times before.

"Whirlawhoomps?" someone called a few minutes later.

"Just the thing!"

"Games afoot!"

One by one, the moths flew off, hurrying out to the grassy lawn to begin a new game.

You see, there are as many different ways of dealing with trouble as there are people in this world. Some people choose to bury their heads deep in the sand. Others prefer to plug their ears and sing loudly until the hardship has passed.

But moths are different. Rather than run from trouble, or sit in a corner and mope, moths will throw themselves into their games. Moths prefer to believe that no matter what the trouble, every bad thing will come right in the end, and in the meantime you ought to try to have a good time.

"Come on, Margaret!" said Pip.

Margaret smiled. Then shaking her worries from her head as best she could, she rose to join them.

CHAPTER 24

A VERY IMPORTANT VISIT

Miss Switch, when faced with life's troubles, would always react in the same way: she would hold a grudge. In fact, grudge holding was one of her greatest talents, and ever since the disaster of the hair tonic she had decided to hold one against the entire world.

An anxious silence had fallen over the orphanage, broken only by the sound of the Matron's moody footfalls coming around a corner and of orphans scampering out of sight like skittish rabbits.

There was no sign that anything would disrupt her nasty mood until two days later, when the telephone rang.

"Good morning, Hopeton Orphanage. This is the Matron speaking," said Miss Switch in her syrupy telephone-answering voice.

"Good morning! It's Hannah calling," said the soft voice of Hannah Tender.

"Hannah. How nice," said Miss Switch. "Does this mean I'm to expect a new arrival at the orphanage?"

"No, I'm calling because I have some rather exciting news," said Hannah.

"Oh?" said the Switch, examining her nail polish.

"I'd love to come by and tell it to you in person."

"Of course. It's always a pleasure."

"Wonderful! I'll see you soon," said Hannah, and she hung up.

Rolling her eyes, Switch went and found her thin, golden whistle. She gave it a halfhearted blow, then yawned. Hannah always did such tiresome things, like talking about philanthropy and hugging the orphans.

Half an hour later when Hannah pulled up to the house in the C.L.C.'s pink car, Miss Switch ushered her onto the porch where an elaborate tea had been laid out.

"How lovely! You really didn't have to, just for me," said Hannah.

"No trouble," said Switch, slouching into her chair. People often say "no trouble" to be polite, but in this case it really had been no trouble. Five dregs had run themselves ragged preparing the tea while Switch took her time selecting the day's outfit. She had settled upon one of her plainer aprons and accessorized it with a dusting of soot across her arms.

"I've just been cleaning the fireplaces," she told Hannah. "The darling orphans are playing in the garden."

This was true, as the orphans had indeed been ordered to play Duck, Duck, Goose by the rosebushes.

But whenever the Pets chose a dreg to be "goose," they would whack them on the head as hard as they could, giving the dreg a nasty headache.

Margaret had already been picked, so as she sat there holding her throbbing head, she concentrated on eavesdropping.

"Wouldn't the children like some of this?" Hannah was saying.

"They've already eaten. Chocolate pancakes with bacon," Switch said. "And fruit," she added.

"Oh, I see," said Hannah, with just a hint of a frown. "Well, I won't keep you in suspense any longer. I'm happy to be the one to tell you, on behalf of the Concerned Ladies' Club, that you have been chosen to receive an Award of Service. You are the Caregiver of the Year!"

At these words, Switch looked up at Hannah in surprise.

"What does that mean?" she said.

"Well, in a few days you'll be given a special medal, and there'll be speeches. All the members of the C.L.C. will be there, and the Mayor, too."

"Oh, Hannah!" said Switch, sitting up straight and beaming. She seemed suddenly much younger. "Goodness me! How very, very kind. How unexpected! Do you think there'll be a photographer?"

Miss Switch had several different smiles. She put them on at different times as it suited her, just like her collection of tattered aprons. There was her motherly smile, which she used in front of the Concerned Ladies and on adoption days. There was her carnivorous smile, which she used to terrorize dregs before bringing them to tears. And there was her dazzling smile, which she used to stupefy clueless members of the public. But this one, rarely seen, was a genuine one. And a genuine smile, especially on someone so beautiful, is hard not to return.

"That's a marvelous idea," said Hannah, smiling back.

A less kind person than Hannah might have felt jealous that she wasn't the one being rewarded for her hard work. But Hannah was the sort of person who felt glad for other people's good fortune. This unselfishness, in Switch's view, was one of her more irritating qualities.

"GOOSE!" came Lacey's violent scream from the garden, followed by a loud cry of pain.

"Well! I'd better let you get back to the children," said Hannah, finishing her tea.

"Yes, they can get a tad boisterous, dear things."

Hannah and Switch said their goodbyes. And Hannah, her head full of ideas for Switch's big day, headed back to the pink car.

But when Hannah looked back over her shoulder to wave, she saw that Switch hadn't moved. The Matron was still standing on the porch, staring out in front of her with a strange look in her eyes.

The youthful look of happiness that had lit up her face a moment before was gone. The look she wore now was fierce and triumphant. It only lasted a second or two before Switch glided down the porch steps toward the garden. And as Hannah drove away down the dusty road, she thought she must have imagined it.

CHAPTER 25

TWO ORPHANS

A long time before our story takes place, another little girl lived in the very same orphanage where our Margaret found herself a prisoner. Just like Margaret, she was not a child praised for her looks, but she had a sweet little heart. Her name was Hannah Tender.

The orphanage was a very different place in Hannah's time. The biggest difference was that there was no tyrannical Matron tormenting children at every waking hour. Instead, the elderly and well-educated Professor Thrumble ran things.

Switch, as you may have noticed, didn't teach the orphans much of anything. The Master, however, thought that textbooks, appendices and dictionaries were the most important things in life.

He had been quite an old man already when the orphanage was built, and by the time Hannah arrived, his bushy eyebrows had turned bright white and his voice was even more gravelly than before. The unfortunate thing was, the older the Master became, the longer and more random his lessons were.

"You there," he would say to Hannah. "Shannon, isn't it? Come along, it's time for a lesson."

Every day he would gather Hannah and the other orphans together, and every day they would have to sit through dreadfully dull lectures about things like the history of the cabbage. He would go on for hours, sometimes long into the night, until the children laid their heads on their desks and fell fast asleep from boredom.

But aside from Professor Thrumble's never-ending lessons, the children of the orphanage were mostly left to themselves.

As Hannah grew older, she began to notice that the pretty little girls and handsome young boys were adopted and taken away from the orphanage while she, for some reason, was always overlooked.

"It is clear to me based on my education that if you were better looking you'd have parents by now," the Master said absently one day. "Why don't you try looking better?"

So Hannah tried to stand up straighter, and comb her hair, and smile as much as she possibly could. Yet still no one chose her. But just like Margaret, Hannah tried to make the best of her situation.

Hannah's best friend was another overlooked girl called Angelica. Angelica had stringy, mud-colored hair, spotty skin and crooked front teeth that were far too big for her mouth. And while beauty may be in the eye of the beholder, there wasn't a single parent who would behold her for more than a few moments before moving their gaze to a more attractive child.

But neither Hannah nor Angelica cared what the other looked like. Together they found little ways to make life in the orphanage more bearable, like passing silly notes to each other during Professor Thrumble's lessons and playing make-believe for hours on end. Their favorite game was imagining what it would be like to be adopted by loving parents and taken to wonderful homes.

"Maybe I could be adopted by a king," Angelica would say. "And I would become a princess."

"Maybe I would have a baby brother or sister who could be my friend," Hannah would say. "And I'd never have to be lonely again."

"Maybe I'll grow up to be beautiful," Angelica would say. "And everyone will love me."

There are many dreams that don't mean a thing. Dreams about taking a ferry to the Arctic to meet the Prime Minister, or being chased around your kindergarten classroom by an angry dentist, for instance, probably mean very little.

But the kind of dream you keep deep inside your heart to remind yourself of what you hope and wish for, the kind of dream you whisper into your pillow every night before you fall asleep — that kind of dream can feed a whole treeful of moths, and it can mean a great deal.

As often happens with children, Hannah and Angelica grew up.

Hannah didn't change very much on the outside. What she did do was make several more good friends among the other orphans and discover that she had a large supply of kindness in her heart.

When new children arrived at the orphanage, Hannah liked nothing more than to make them feel welcome. She would walk with them to the Master's lectures, or sit with them at mealtimes, or smile at them when she passed them in the hall.

Unlike Hannah, Angelica changed a lot on the outside. For one thing, her mouth grew to make room for her teeth, which no longer looked quite so large or crooked. And when Angelica discovered that the other orphans had stopped picking on her as a result, it gave her a wonderful feeling. So while Hannah was off making new friends, Angelica was busy going through each of her features and thinking of ways she could improve them.

When Hannah and Angelica were old enough to set out on their own, Hannah moved to the very town where you first saw her and found a job in philanthropy. This allowed her to keep helping children as lonesome as she had once been, which filled her life with happiness.

But Angelica moved to a big city, where she got a job at a dressmaker's shop. As soon as she had saved enough money, she bought herself a mouthful of braces to straighten out her teeth, and expensive skin cream to smooth out her complexion, and every other product she could think of that might help her appearance. When she had saved up some more money, she went to a beauty parlor and had her mud-colored hair dyed blonde.

And when she began to notice people stopping in their tracks just to stare at her, she knew that the thing she had dreamed of every night of her life had come true.

She had grown up beautiful.

Have you put the pieces together? Can you guess what happened next to the orphan called Angelica, one day as she was on her way to work?

"Excusez-moi!" said a glamorous woman, rushing up to her on the street.

"What's your name, dah-ling?" said a man with a ponytail who was with her.

"It's Angelica," said Angelica. "Angelica Switch."

You see, no one pops into the world filled with fury and hate, like a rotten wormy apple. Just as every story has a villain, every villain has a story. Sometimes the rottenness seeps in slowly over many lonesome years. But other times, through the words of a cruel photographer and the sudden loss of a dream, it rushes in all at once, like water through a broken dam.

These were the memories that were flitting around in Miss Switch's mind as she watched Hannah's car drive off down the dusty road. But instead of paying them any attention, she brushed them away as if they were nothing more than bothersome cobwebs, and didn't think of them again.

CHAPTER 26

THE DERANGEMENT OF TOBY BOBBINS

When something happens that is the exact opposite of what you would expect, that is called irony.

The *Titanic* being nicknamed "Unsinkable" was ironic, because the last thing you'd expect an unsinkable ship to do is spring a leak on her first voyage at sea. Chopping off your hair and selling it to a wigmaker to buy your best friend a new baseball is ironic if your friend just sold her bat to buy you a new hairbrush.

Miss Switch being given an award for Caregiver of the Year was ironic because, as you know, Miss Switch was unfit to care for a tomato plant, much less a child.

But Miss Switch was untroubled by irony. Even when she was to be given an award for kindness, she had no problem acting as unkindly as possible. So the very next morning when Lacey bounded up the stairs yelling that Toby Bobbins had ruined the Matron's best silk dress in the laundry tubs, Switch emerged from her room feeling just as unkind as ever.

Working the tubs was one of the worst jobs a dreg could get. There were ten massive tubs deep in the bowels of the orphanage, each with a wooden step-ladder that wobbled when you went up it. On tub duty, the first thing you had to do was pour soap and bleach and chemicals into the scalding water, then try not to burn yourself as you loaded in the dirty clothes. Once this was done, you had to stand for hours in the steamy, smelly basement, stirring the tubs with a long wooden paddle to make sure everything washed evenly.

Toby, who had been working the tubs for a good four hours that morning, had become so tired and dizzy from the smell of bleach that he'd fallen asleep at his post and forgotten to stir the delicate clothes.

When Switch stepped into the laundry room and saw her expensive dress reduced to a dripping pile of tatters, she was secretly delighted. This may seem like a very odd reaction, as Switch dearly loved owning pretty and expensive things. But the more important truth about Switch was this: she loved cruelty more.

Switch was an artist when it came to punishment, and as her glittering eyes took in the sight of chubby Toby Bobbins and the ruined silk dress, she knew that he was just the inspiration she needed.

"So," she said sweetly to the red-faced Toby. "You've had yourself a nice little nap, I hear. You're probably feeling very refreshed."

Toby gave a very small nod.

"I don't see that you'll be needing to sleep anymore, will you?" Switch said.

"Not right now, Miss Switch," said Toby meekly.

"Not ever," smiled the Switch.

And from that moment on, Toby was forbidden to sleep.

Switch shut him in a cupboard in the basement, and the Pets were set on a nightly schedule to take turns keeping him awake by poking at him with a long stick whenever he closed his eyes.

This went on for two nights in a row. And on the morning of the third day, the day of Switch's award ceremony, when Margaret and Judy brought Toby his breakfast mush, they found him sitting on the floor with an aluminum pot on his head, singing quietly.

"What do you do with a drunken sailor, just as the sun was ri-sing," warbled Toby. He stared at Judy, cross-eyed. "Captain!"

"Oh, no!" Judy gasped in horror. "He's gone off the edge!"

"Hey, non-nonny!" sang Toby. "Nifty nonny puffs!"

And then, without taking even a bite of his breakfast, he closed his eyes, fell flat on the floor and started snoring. No amount of poking and kicking and pinching from the Pets could wake him again.

News of the breakdown reached Switch, who interrupted her beauty preparations to pay a special visit to Toby's cupboard. When she saw how successful her punishment had been, she was absolutely delighted. Laughing as if the whole thing were a marvelous joke, she waved a hand at Margaret and Judy to have them carry Toby up to his bed.

That laugh of Switch's and that casual wave of her hand were so unfeeling that Margaret couldn't stand it. She had never been so angry in her entire life.

Anger was one of the many things Great-aunt Linda hadn't approved of, along with idle hands and poor table manners. But anger is a perfectly natural emotion, and sometimes it can tell you very important things.

As Margaret carried Toby up the stairs, she saw the pitiful way his tongue lolled out of his open mouth. She heard the distant peals of Switch's laughter. And her anger told her she had to do something.

As every other dreg trudged down to the basement to begin a massive laundry scrubbing for Switch's big day, Margaret slipped away. And when she was sure no one was looking, she ran out into the bright afternoon, heading for the moth tree.

CHAPTER 27

THE WAKING OF THE MOTHS

If you have lived any significant amount of time in this world, you will have noticed that different things come naturally to different types of creatures.

It is in the nature of a spotted woodpecker, for example, to munch on grubs and worms and to enjoy it immensely, just as it is in the nature of grubs and worms to be munched on by spotted woodpeckers and not to enjoy the experience quite so much. It is in the nature of small infants to cry and make a ruckus whenever they are hungry or moist, just as it is in the nature of airplane passengers to cry and make a ruckus whenever they are seated next to small infants. These are simply the rules of nature.

There are also some things that do not come naturally. It is not in the nature of small girls, for example, to hear the tiniest and quietest of noises.

And it is not in the nature of moths to awaken in broad daylight and tinker in the affairs of humans.

But there are always exceptions to the rules.

When Margaret came scrambling through the thorny tunnel, the moths of the tree were fast asleep, and try as she might, she couldn't rouse them.

"Flit!" she cried, as she caught sight of the sleeping moth. "Rimblewisp! Everyone, wake up!" But not a single moth stirred.

Finally, she caught sight of Pip's familiar gray wings.

"Pip!" she cried, shaking the branch where he slept. "Wake up! Oh, wake up!"

Pip twitched, and mumbled, "Hmm?"

"Pipperflit!" Margaret shouted.

"Margaret?" Pip murmured, looking blearily up at her. "You're early. Why don't you come back later …"

And he laid his head back down on the branch.

"Pip! Don't go back to sleep," Margaret said quickly. "Listen to me. I know what's been happening to the Nimblers! It's Switch!"

"The Switch …" muttered Pip.

"Yes, she's been turning them sour by tormenting us dregs!"

"Wait," said Pip with a shake of his head. "Did you say Nimblers?"

"Yes!" said Margaret. "We need to get rid of Miss Switch, and then the Nimblers will go back to the way they used to be. Remember, Pip? Licorice and berries and honey? But I need your help, you and all the moths. Help me wake them up!"

"You can count on me, Margaret," Pip said with a yawn, nodding his head. "Down with the dungwaddler!" But then he looked around at the sleeping moths, flicking his wings uncertainly. "Only ... moths don't wake up in the daytime."

"Pip," said Margaret, an idea forming in her mind. "Look at it like a game. The very greatest game you've ever played. A game to bring back the good Nimblers."

At this, Pip perked up. His wings began to twitch. Then he flew up into the air.

"*Games afoot!*" he cried. "Everyone up! All moths up for the Greatest Game!"

The tree began to stir, and the moths to grumble.

"What's going on?"

"Go back to sleep, Pip. We'll play tonight."

"The Greatest Game! The Greatest Game of all!" Pip cried. "It's happening right now! And the prize is a whopping great load of Nimblers — the most tastiest Nimblers you could possibly chase down! Enough for everyone!"

Now the tree began to rustle, as the moths began murmuring all at once.

"What's he saying?"

"Nimblers?"

"The Greatest Game!"

"Everyone!" Margaret called out over the noise,

staring up at the crowd of tiny faces. "This will be a game you'll never forget for the rest of your lives, and you only get to play it once. If you win, it will be just as Pip said."

The hum in the tree grew into a quiet roar.

And then, high up in the branches, a single voice cried, "For Nimblers!"

"All right, Whatsit!" called Flit.

"Now listen carefully!" Margaret said. "Here's what we're going to do."

CHAPTER 28

THE RALLYING OF
THE DREGS

In preparation for the awards ceremony, Miss Switch had tripled her usual beauty regime. She had powdered and primped. She had creamed and curled. She had tucked and trimmed.

She had spent hours picking an outfit that was the perfect combination of modesty and grace, and her final selection was now lying neatly on her bed. As the hour of her triumph drew near, she sat at her vanity table wearing a wrinkle-reducing face cream and practicing her acceptance speech in her head.

But as Switch was smiling smugly at her reflection, a very different kind of preparation was underway outdoors.

Just outside the orphanage, crouched quietly next to the side door, Margaret was waiting. When a small gray moth came flying toward her a moment later, she rose.

"The dregs are in the underground," said Pip, coming to land on her shoulder.

"The basement, you mean?" said Margaret.

"That's the one. That wonky-nosed Pet is guarding them."

"And the others?" Margaret asked.

"Sneaking snacks," said Pip.

Margaret nodded. Switch had ordered the dregs to rewash every piece of clothing and linen in the house so that everything would be extra clean for the photographer. And since none of the Pets wanted the job of keeping an eye on them in the steamy room, guard duty had fallen on the dreggish Pet, Agatha Spink.

"I think I know what to do," said Margaret.

Treading softly, she crept through the door into the orphanage. Pip flew ahead to check on the Pets, who were now at the long carved table in the dining room.

"All clear!" he called.

Margaret darted into the kitchen and, rummaging in the pantry, quickly gathered up two large handfuls of cookies. Then before the Pets even knew she had been there, she was gone.

Keeping out of sight, she made her way to the basement stairs. When she reached the bottom, she found a pouting, fidgeting Agatha Spink, leaning unhappily against the doorway of the laundry room.

Unfortunately, things had not much improved for Agatha since her efforts to win over Miss Switch. She still spent her days wishing she fitted in. She still spent her nights afraid of being tossed out in the cold. Through it all, she had grown to be the most miserable of all the orphans.

"Hey!" she shouted when she saw Margaret approaching. "You're supposed to be in there, with the others!" Then, realizing it was Margaret she was talking to, she clapped a hand over her mouth in horror.

"Miss Switch sent these down for you," Margaret said immediately, holding up the cookies with a smile. "She wants you to know that she really appreciates all the hard work you're doing, even though she sometimes doesn't show it. Anyway, I have to get back to work now."

Without giving Agatha a moment to object, Margaret pressed the cookies into her hands, strode purposefully into the laundry room and shut the door behind her. Though her heart was racing, Margaret knew that Agatha, standing wide-eyed and open-mouthed in the hallway, had believed her, if only because she so deeply wanted to.

But Margaret didn't have time to feel glad or proud or relieved just yet. Her real challenge was still to come.

All around her, the dregs of the orphanage were stirring steaming pots of laundry. Their faces were red with heat, their clothes were stained with sweat, and their arms and legs had broken out in splotches where the boiling water had splashed up and burned them.

Gathering her courage, Margaret took two steps into the room.

Starting a revolution is a tricky thing. Usually, kings or

emperors or elementary-school teachers who go around stomping on their subjects do such a good job of it that the subjects never even think of standing up to them. A very good speech is sometimes needed to get things going. And a very good speech was what Margaret had to make now, as she stood with Pip on her shoulder, looking around at the downtrodden dregs.

"Go on, Margaret!" said Pip.

Margaret cleared her throat.

"Everyone," she said. "I have something to say."

The dregs closest to her looked up in shock, then turned back to their work quickly. Margaret glanced at Pip, who flicked his wings encouragingly.

She took a deep breath, walked to an overturned bucket in the center of the room and stood on top of it.

"Dregs!" she said as loudly as she could.

A few more dregs looked up, but most of them pretended they hadn't heard her.

"Listen to me!" cried Margaret. "For too long we have suffered under the rule of the Switch!"

The splashing of the paddles quieted as several dregs stopped their stirring.

"We've scrubbed and cleaned and cooked, and what has it brought us?"

"Nothing," said quiet Timothy Smealing, and a few more dregs turned to listen.

"Nothing," agreed Margaret. "Nothing but pinches and punishments. Nothing but taunts and torment. And it's worse than it's ever been."

Now the whole room was watching her, and several of the dregs were nodding.

"Think of Sarah Pottley! Think of Toby! Think of everything she's done to each of you," Margaret cried. "The time has come to act. We can't let Switch push us around for one more second."

"That's right," said Phoebe Frizzleton. "It's not fair!"

"She needs to be stopped," said Bessie Blotchly.

Margaret nodded firmly. "We've got to show the world Switch's true colors."

"But how can we?" said Judy, her eyes wide. "No one's ever managed to do it before."

"I'm talking about joining forces," said Margaret. "The Switch is getting an award today. A lot of people will be visiting the orphanage. We're going to make sure that they see her the way we see her, and that she can't talk her way out of it. Everyone will need to help if it's going to work. So, are we in this together?"

For a moment, no one spoke.

"We're with you, Margaret!" Vickram suddenly cried, his eyes shining.

"Yeah!" cried the rest of the dregs.

"Tell us what you need us to do!" piped Timothy Smealing.

"Right," said Margaret. "Bessie Blotchly, I need you to go up on the roof and sit by the chimney. When you get the signal, I want you to start knocking on it. Phoebe Frizzleton, you and Vickram will have to take care of Agatha Spink. Make sure she doesn't raise the alarm.

Helen and Timothy, in exactly ten minutes, gather the rest of the dregs and wait in the front hall for when the grown-ups come. No more games and smiles this time."

"Got it," said Bessie Blotchly.

"Aye, aye!" said Phoebe Frizzleton.

"We're with you, Margaret!" said Helen Ravish.

"And Judy," Margaret said. "You're with me. We're going to take care of the Pets."

Judy looked nervous, but nodded bravely.

"Okay, everyone," Margaret said. "Let's go!"

And as if she had just blown the Switch's golden whistle, the dregs burst through the basement door.

"But Margaret," Judy said, as the pair of them passed a hollering Agatha Spink being pushed into a broom cupboard, "there's no way the two of us are any match for all the Pets."

"It's not just the two of us," Margaret said. "Just wait and see."

CHAPTER 29

PETS, PETRIFIED

If Margaret had mentioned that her great plan rested on nothing more than a treeful of small gray moths, Judy might have been less willing to "just wait and see." But Margaret didn't mention it, because Judy didn't yet know one very important fact: that small creatures are sometimes capable of great things.

"Wait here," Margaret said. "As soon as you see me coming around the corner, call for Lacey as loud as you can."

Judy nodded.

Margaret slipped down the hall and around the corner to an open window.

"All right, Pip," said Margaret. "It's time. Send up the signal."

"Right!" cried Pip, flicking his wings with excitement. Flying out the window, he zipped around in three big loop-de-loops. Margaret held her breath, staring out at the yard.

Sure enough, after only a moment, she saw the slightest movement of another tiny moth rising up from the vegetable garden. The moth returned Pip's loop-de-loop signal, then came zooming toward the window.

"Here they come!" cried Pip, landing on the sill near Margaret.

The new moth came zipping through the window, and was followed by another. Then another. And then a hundred more! Soon the air was filled with an enormous stream of moths, flying right through the window and coming to land at Margaret's feet. She could hear their tiny laughing voices, saying, "Right, Finkripple," and "The Greatest Game!" and "Whizwinger, watch my foot!"

"All right, moths," Margaret whispered. "Form up!"

"Right!" called the moths.

With a flurry of wings, a group of about twenty moths fluttered into a flat circular formation about the size of a dinner plate and landed on the floor. Once they'd done that, a second group gathered to flutter right above them, making another plate-sized layer. Groups of moths continued to pile one on top of the other, fluttering above the moths below them, until the column of moths was a head taller than Margaret herself.

The sight was astonishing to behold! The tower of moths fluttered and wiggled and swayed like some strange sea creature.

"Perfect!" said Margaret. "Is everyone ready?"

"Ready!" called the moths.

Margaret ran back around the corner and waved at Judy.

"Lacey!" Judy began yelling. "Come quick! Lacey!"

Margaret only had time to whisper "Don't worry, they're on our side" to Judy before the monstrous moth creature appeared around the corner, swaying and floating slowly toward them.

"Yikes!" screamed Judy in real fear. "Lacey, Pets, *hurry*!"

A moment later, Lacey herself appeared.

"What is it, dreg?" she shouted at Judy, looking ready to pummel her. But then her eye caught sight of the massive beast at the end of the hall.

Just as it is rather satisfying to see nasty tyrants get a taste of their own medicine, it is extremely pleasant to see someone who has spent her whole life scaring people have her own wits scared silly.

Lacey shrieked, jumped in the air and began running in circles and screaming. The sound of Lacey screaming in fear was something that had never been heard before within the walls of the Hopeton Orphanage, and the noise drew the rest of the Pets to the hallway in an instant. When they saw the swaying moth tower, they followed Lacey's example and began to scream, too.

"What is *that*?!" they shrieked.

"Goodness!" said Margaret loudly. "It's a carnivorous Flapdragon! I've read about them. They're so deadly that one bite will kill you in a heartbeat."

This news made Lacey even more hysterical, and as she ran in circles she started screaming, "What do we do? What do we *do*?!"

"The Flapdragon can't open doors!" Margaret cried.

"Quick, the bedroom! You'll be safe in there!"

Margaret didn't need to say another word. The Pets stampeded into their bedroom like a herd of antelopes fleeing from a hungry lion.

"Do you want me to shut the door?" Margaret asked them.

"Yes!" cried the Pets. "Shut it! Shut it quickly!"

"Shall I lock it, too, just to be safe?"

"*Yes!*" screamed the Pets. "For goodness' sake, lock it!"

"Okay," said Margaret. Slamming the door shut with a satisfying bang, she lowered the latch, and the Pets were trapped.

Margaret smiled and nodded to the moths, who fell away from their tower and fluttered all around her in a great cheering cloud.

"Thanks, everyone!" she whispered. "We did it!"

"Anytime, Margaret!" said the chorus of voices. "On to the next!"

And in a jumble of loop-de-loops, they headed back out the open window.

"It worked!" laughed Pip, landing on Margaret's shoulder.

"*Moths!*" breathed Judy. "That was amazing! I never knew moths could do a thing like that!"

"Yes," said Margaret. "Moths can do all sorts of things."

But she didn't tell Judy anything more right then, for there was still work to be done.

With pounding hearts, the two orphans and the moth headed straight for the bedroom of the Switch.

CHAPTER 30

THE GREATEST GAME

For anyone who didn't know better, the simple wooden door to Switch's private sitting room might not have looked like anything much.

Most people wouldn't have noticed the rich polish of the wood or the shine of the silver doorknob, or paused to smell the expensive perfumes wafting from inside. Most people would never have suspected that the door hid anything very remarkable.

But as Margaret, Pip and Judy reached the end of Switch's corridor, they noticed all these things, and they knew that what was waiting for them behind the door must be very remarkable indeed.

"All right, Pip," Margaret said. "This is it."

Judy stared open-mouthed as, on cue, Pip flew from Margaret's shoulder and crept under the door.

"All clear!" he called from inside.

Margaret nodded at Judy and slowly turned the silver

knob. The door opened with the tiniest of squeaks, and Margaret and Judy slipped inside.

A dazzling sight met their eyes.

Switch's sitting room had three layers of Turkish rugs, tapestries on the walls, and dozens of vases, statues and candelabras. Margaret recognized some of them from her very first day in the orphanage when they had decorated the ground floor. Just like a magpie hoarding shiny objects in its nest, Switch had greedily gathered all the treasures of the house for her own enjoyment.

Moving farther into the room, Margaret and Judy came to another door, this one painted bright gold, and with a crystal knob. It was a door lavish enough for a queen. The door to Switch's bedroom.

Margaret put her eye to the keyhole and squinted.

The room was filled with clothes, shoes, hats, handbags and jewelry — gold and silver, diamonds and pearls. Switch had stuffed the high-ceilinged room so full that it looked like the den of a fashionable dragon. Stacks of glossy magazines were crammed wherever they could fit, and on every wall was a mirror, which made the hoard seem even bigger.

"I can hear her unscrewing a jar," Margaret whispered.

"It's such an important day," Judy whispered back. "I bet she wants to look extra beautiful."

"Pip, can you get a closer look?"

"'Course," said Pip. He crept through the crack under the door. "Yep," he said. "She's putting stuff on her face. Looks like she's almost finished."

"It's time," Margaret said to Judy, who hadn't heard any of that. "Judy, go to the roof and give Phoebe the signal." Judy nodded and darted from the room.

"Okay, Pip," Margaret whispered. "Send the alert."

What happened next inside the room would have made the most serious person you know burst out laughing.

Miss Switch was sitting at her vanity table wearing a girlish blue dress that puffed out at her knees in a very charming way. She was just putting a delicate pink blush on the apples of her cheeks when a strange knocking sound drifted down from the chimney at the other side of the room. When the knocking continued, she frowned, walked over to the fireplace, and stuck her head in to investigate.

As she peered up the chimney, the knocking was joined by other sounds: a scraping noise, and a soft sort of fluttering. Bewildered, she stuck her head farther in. Before she knew what was happening, before she could even think about pulling herself back, a gigantic puff of black soot came shooting down from up above.

"Eeugh!" cried the Matron, covering her eyes with her hands and hacking. The soot was plastered across her face. It was buried in her golden hair. It was stuck in her teeth, and in her eyelashes, and up her nose, and smudged all across the front of her dress.

She broke into a sneezing fit, staggering backwards.

But this indignity was only the beginning.

"Games afoot!" came a mothish voice that Margaret could hear and the Switch could not.

Zooming down the chimney and out of the fireplace came a moth, covered in dark soot.

"Get away!" Switch shrieked, as it flew straight toward her and started flapping around her head.

But the moth did not get away. And to Switch's horror, a hundred more of the sooty moths came flying from the chimney, encircling her in a cloud of fluttering gray wings.

Dipping their feet in an open pot of face cream, one by one the moths swooped down to land on her, leaving gooey footprints across her face and arms. Flailing her arms in a panic, Switch began to shriek and run from one side of the room to the other.

Through it all, Margaret watched at the keyhole.

"She's on the run!" said Pip, squeezing under the door. "That's your cue."

Margaret began knocking loudly on the Matron's door.

"Miss Switch!" she called. "Is everything all right? I heard a scream."

The bedroom door swung open, and it took every ounce of Margaret's self-control not to burst out laughing.

The Matron stood in the doorway, covered from head to toe with dust and soot and goo. Her hair was sticking out wildly and her eyes were bulging with fear.

"Bugs!" cried the Switch frantically. "My room is infested!" And then, seeing who it was standing at the door, she tried to compose herself.

"Dreg! Get in there right now and fix it."

Margaret dashed into the room, and the moths circled around her, cheering.

"I tagged its nose!" said one.

"I got it on the bum!" said another.

"I think we're winning!" said another.

"Ten points!" cried another, who sounded like Flit.

Margaret smiled at the circling moths and gave a quick nod toward Switch's open window.

At her signal, a second wave of moths came swooping in through the window. Unlike the others, they were free from soot, but each was carrying a long silken string with a single caterpillar hanging from the bottom.

"Hi, Margaret!" called the caterpillars.

A moment later the moths had landed on Switch's jewelry case, and the caterpillars set to work fastening their threads to her ropes of pearls and diamonds. When the moths took flight again, the jewels took flight with them, hanging from the bottoms of the silken threads. For while a single moth is just strong enough to carry one small blue Plurpil, hundreds of moths can carry much more.

"Oh no!" Margaret called out. "Miss Switch, your jewels!"

When Switch turned to look, what she saw made her blood run cold. The vile bugs were flying toward the window, carrying off her glittering necklaces.

"Thieves!" bellowed the Switch. "I'm being *robbed*!"

"Quick," Margaret cried. "We have to catch them!"

With a nod at the moths, she began grabbing the

jewels from the air. Switch hesitated, then darted back across the room. And with the triumphant cheers of the moths spurring her on, Margaret began draping layers of necklaces around the Matron's long neck.

"Faster, dreg!" Switch screeched, as Margaret hurried to empty the jewelry case.

"That's everything!" she said.

Without so much as a glance in Margaret's direction, the soot-covered Switch ran from the room, leaving Margaret to hurry along behind her.

Through the orphanage they went, through the ornate sitting room, past the bedrooms of the orphans and down the front stairs. But when they reached the bottom, Switch froze. The dregs were waiting for her in the front hall.

There was shocked silence for several moments as the dregs stared at the grimy, goggle-eyed Matron. Then from somewhere in the crowd came a tiny giggle. The giggle spread and grew, and soon the entire room was giggling, then laughing, then roaring at the sooty sight before them.

"Quiet!" hissed the Switch in her threateningly low voice.

But the roar of the dregs kept getting louder.

"Stop laughing right now! Stop it or I'll feed you all to the hobos!" she shouted.

But her threats were drowned out by the glee of the children. Several of them had fallen to the ground with laughter and were kicking their feet in the air.

Rage filled Switch's heart, and as she stared around at the orphans in fury, her gaze fell on Judy giggling loudly near the front of the group.

"I SAID QUIET!" Switch screamed hysterically, and grabbing Judy by the arm, she lifted her high in the air.

"Don't!" cried Margaret, grabbing hold of Switch's other arm to stop her.

But Switch threw Margaret off wildly and began to shake poor Judy.

"How dare you laugh at me?! You're worthless! You're pointless! You're nothing but a *dreg!*"

Just as she raised a hand to strike the dangling girl, a different sound cut through all the laughter and screaming and chaos.

"MISS SWITCH!"

The voice was loud and booming, and as the children all turned toward it, they saw standing in the front door the commanding presence of the Sheriff.

And standing just behind him, staring in at the dreadful scene, were Gertrude, Prudie, Hannah, a dozen townspeople and three newspaper reporters with flashbulb cameras.

CHAPTER 31

THE UNMASKING

Do you know the feeling you get right before a china plate smashes to the ground? Unless you are in a Greek restaurant, this is a very tense sort of feeling to have. It was just this feeling that hung in the air for a split second before the cameras began madly flashing at the soot-covered, orphan-shaking, bejeweled Miss Switch.

At first Switch didn't seem to be able to move. She stood frozen in her bizarre pose and stared back at the shocked people in the doorway. But then she dropped Judy and turned to the Sheriff.

"Sheriff, I can explain!" she gasped.

This time, it was Margaret who wouldn't let *her* finish.

"She's a thief!" Margaret cried.

The Hopetoners gasped, and Margaret took a step forward.

"She's stolen all your money to buy those jewels, and she treats us like slaves!"

"It's true!" cried the other orphans.

"She starves us!"

"She tortures us!"

"She calls us dregs!"

Every orphan in the hall was nodding and holding up bruised, pinched arms.

"No!" Switch cried desperately. "The dear children are only joking with you. We were playing a game, you see, and I was playing the wicked witch."

But the Sheriff's face had darkened. "There's nothing worse than a thief," he said, shaking his head. "But you, Miss Switch, are a thief *and* a liar."

The white-haired Mayor Picklewort emerged from the crowd, clutching a golden trophy. "We can't give an award to a thieving liar!"

"I should think not, Harold!" said Gertrude. "It would be the absolute *opposite* of procedure!"

"How could someone so beautiful do something so dreadful?" asked Prudie, looking horrified.

"Margaret!" said Hannah, running inside to pull Margaret into a hug. "I'm so sorry I didn't believe you!"

In another moment, the rest of the crowd had rushed into the house to hug and comfort the other orphans.

"Poor little ragamuffins!" they cried.

"Such sweet little things!"

Some of the townspeople found that they didn't want to stop hugging the orphans, and so they adopted them on the spot.

One couple fell instantly in love with poor, brave Judy

and asked her if she wanted them for parents, which she did. Sarah Pottley went home with a lonely lady whose children were all grown up and living far away. And bleary-eyed Toby Bobbins, who had finally woken from his long sleep and come stumbling down the stairs, captured the heart of a plump grandmotherly woman. She asked him to be her new son, and he agreed, so long as laundry wasn't one of his chores.

The remaining townspeople turned their attention to Miss Switch.

"Despicable!" muttered one well-dressed lady in a fancy hat. "To think that all our generous donations went right into her greedy hands!"

"It's unthinkable," said old Mayor Picklewort. "After all our good philanthropy! Don't anyone tell the Munsfielders about this."

The Concerned Ladies were the most horrified of all.

"This calls for an emergency meeting," said Prudie.

"It's not in the schedule," Gertrude said, checking her day planner. "But I suppose we can make an exception. Our first order of business will be to decide what to do with the Caregiver of the Year Award. It would seem very ironic to give it to Miss Switch, under the circumstances."

"Shouldn't we decide what to do about the orphans first?" said Hannah. "They're going to need someone to look after them."

"Yes, she's right," said Prudie. "Children mustn't be left without supervision."

"I'll put an ad in the newspaper right away," said Gertrude.

"That won't be necessary," said Hannah. "I'd like to volunteer for the job."

Gertrude and Prudie looked at her in surprise.

"But you're not well educated," said Gertrude. "How will you teach the children about economics?"

"And you're not very glamorous," said Prudie. "How will the children look up to you?"

"I think I'll manage," said Hannah. "Don't you agree, children?"

With a great roar of joy, the children agreed. And right then and there, Hannah Tender was declared the new Matron of the Hopeton Orphanage.

And what of the soot-smeared Switch? The Miss Switch who had once been so beautiful and terrifying?

She seemed to have deflated completely. As she stood there staring at the hall full of embracing adults and children, she felt utterly unimportant. The Sheriff took her by the arm and led her away, and none of the orphans ever saw her face again.

And as beautiful and villainous as Angelica Switch had become, she looked in that moment more like the ugly little orphan she had once been, alone and ignored.

CHAPTER 32

ON ENDINGS

Writers, philosophers and great-aunts have said a great many things about endings. Things like, "All's well that ends well" and "Every end is a new beginning" and "When you close a door, you open a window." But when endings happen to people in real life, no one gives much thought to all ending well, or new beginnings, or doors and windows. This is because people's lives are far too untidy for real endings and beginnings.

It is better, perhaps, to simply say what happened.

The Nimblers that floated above the Hopeton Orphanage that first night were sweeter than they had ever been. The moths zoomed and careened and twirled about, drinking in the wild, delicious flavors until the sun came up. Then they fluttered contentedly back to their tree, hiccupping and dizzy. And from that night on, the story of the Greatest Game was told again and again, with new heroic details added at every telling.

Hannah became a very good Matron, just as you might have supposed. Her first order of business was the Pets, who were raving hysterically about a monster in the hallway, and whom Hannah sent straight to bed with cold compresses. Then Switch's hoard of treasures was sold, and the money was used to buy the clothes and books and toys that the poor trusting mailman thought he'd been delivering all along. Mush was banned from the menu, and the orphans were at last given some education, though not so much as to put them to sleep.

Every so often, Hannah did pay a visit to her old schoolmate Angelica. She was the only visitor Switch ever had, and it was hard, at first, to find anything to talk about. But slowly, as time went by, Hannah began to recognize her old friend again. The bleach grew out of Switch's hair, and her makeup didn't seem so heavy as before. While Hannah was never quite sure if her visits were wholly welcome, over time Switch's rude remarks did seem to lessen. Eventually, the two of them could sit together, if not comfortably, at least cordially.

And the life of Margaret Grey, which had been so quiet and so unusual, became more like other children's lives.

As soon as the other orphans didn't have to pretend she was invisible, Margaret made friends.

There were still unpleasant people like Lacey to deal with, but they lost their taste for bullying somewhat when they found that bad behavior now earned them extra chores.

Margaret's world became louder than it had ever been. After ten years without any brothers or sisters, she now had lots of people to shout and scream and holler with. And as Hannah encouraged outdoor games on fine afternoons, there was a lot of hollering to be had.

If this were a proper world, Margaret would have surely gained all these delightful things and still have been able to keep the good parts of her old life. Her retreats to the moth tree would have been filled with the happiness that spilled over from her everyday life.

But no one can live between two worlds forever, however much they might like to.

The more friends Margaret made, the more she ran and played and laughed, the harder it was for her to hear the tiny sounds that used to come so easily to her. And though she still snuck off every night to visit the moths, their voices were growing quieter and quieter.

One afternoon as the orphans were whooping through the yard in a loud game of tag, a car pulled up on the dusty road, and from inside came a kind-looking woman and a man with a warm smile.

Within an hour, Margaret's life had taken a very wonderful new turn. And a few minutes later, her cheeks aching from so many smiles, Margaret ran as fast as she could to the moth tree.

"Pip!" she called as she rushed inside. "Pip, wake up! I've been adopted!"

Pip fluttered sleepily down from the upper branches

of the tree and dropped into the palm of Margaret's open hand.

"By parents?" he cried.

"Yes!" said Margaret.

Margaret beamed, and Pip congratulated, and it was the happiest either of them had ever been.

"You'll come, won't you?" said Margaret, after a minute. "You'll come live in town, too?"

"Oh!" said Pip. "But Margaret, I couldn't live in a town."

"What do you mean?" said Margaret. "Of course you could. It can be like an adventure!"

"An awfully big one …" Pip said, and his voice was so quiet that the blowing of the wind almost blocked it out.

Margaret opened her mouth to argue, but then she looked at her friend and saw, for the first time in a very long time, just how small a creature he was. And then her throat felt very tight.

It is an inconvenient thing, in moments when you most need to tell someone something, that your eyes begin to burn and words seem to get stuck in your throat. Margaret wanted to tell Pip many things: how he and the moths had saved them all; how, if not for them, she would have had a very different life. But she could only manage to say one thing.

"I'll remember you always," said Margaret. "You're my first friend."

She could barely hear Pip's next words, and she had to concentrate every bit of her energy on her ears just to make them out. When she did, they were barely louder than the rustle of the leaves.

"And you're my Margaret."

She looked down at the small gray creature in her hand, and he looked up at her. Leaning forward, she gave him a soft kiss on the tip of his wing, and he tilted his head to her. Then he did three fantastic loop-de-loops in the air and flew up into the treetop.

When Margaret crawled through the brush and out into the day, she ran into the open arms of her new parents. They drove down the dusty road away from the orphanage, away from the waving orphans and Hannah's smiling face, and away from the tree that held Margaret's secret. And that was the first day of what would be a very loving and wonderful new life.

But whenever Margaret saw a pair of tiny wings flutter by, or touched the bark of a gnarled old tree, she thought of her first friend.

Whenever she felt lonely or sad, she would go to a green place, away from the clatter and noise of the city. She would close her eyes, and she would stay very still. And she would listen.

And sometimes, from very far off, she could swear she heard the laughing voices of the moths.